LAST STAND AT THE BATHROOM CORRAL

I watched my son and Leonie with fascination. It came as a shock to me that I was witnessing the possible birth of a family. So *this* was what most people did.

A cold sweat crept over me. Oh my God. I was becoming a family man. What happened to me? I used to be perfectly content with my life. Now, in a few short weeks, my life had turned upside down. Panic set in and for a moment I thought I was going to hyperventilate.

I left Leonie and Louis at the table and headed for the men's room. All of the sudden, I needed some space. I found a quiet stall and sat down on the toilet fully clothed.

"'Scuse me." A deep voice interrupted my meditation. "I'm looking for Dakota Bombay."

That's weird. Someone trailed me into the men's room?

"I'll be out in a second." I stood up quietly, sliding my leather belt out of the loops on my Dockers.

Then the door slammed open, knocking me back...

Other *Making It* titles by Leslie Langtry:

'SCUSE ME WHILE I KILL THIS GUY

Guns Will Keep Us Together

Leslie Langtry

Making it

NEW YORK CITY

*This book is dedicated to the memory of my
loving father and gifted teacher—Lawrence
Roe Cederoth. He introduced me to James
Bond, Ray Bradbury and Batman—all
of whom influence my writing every day.
Thanks, Larry. I love and miss you.*

A MAKING IT Book®

February 2008

Published by

Dorchester Publishing Co., Inc.
200 Madison Avenue
New York, NY 10016

ISBN 10: 0-8439-6036-1
ISBN 13: 978-0-8439-6036-5

The name "Making It" and its logo are trademarks of
Dorchester Publishing Co., Inc.

Printed in the United States of America.

10 9 8 7 6 5 4 3 2 1

Visit us on the web at www.dorchesterpub.com.

ACKNOWLEDGMENTS

I'd like to thank my incredible editor, Leah, my fabulous agent, Kristin, my amazing husband, Tom and my super-talented children, Margaret & Jack and the rest of my family (the Cederoths, Johnsons, Smileys, Boquets and Thompsons), the Scoobies, Girl Scout Troop #8630 (you guys rock!) and my fabulous friends Michelle & Bernie Sapp—who generously loaned me their son, Ian, for this book.

Guns Will Keep Us Together

Chapter One

"The Addams Family credo: *'Sic gorgiamus allos subjectatos nunc.'* We gladly feast on those who would subdue us. Not just pretty words."
— Morticia Addams, *The Addams Family*

Getting a phone call can be a good thing. It could be someone calling to inform you of an inheritance, or that cute blonde you met last night begging for another round of find-the-kielbasa.

On the other hand, it could be the doctor calling to tell you that you did, indeed, pick up an intestinal parasite while in Uruguay, or the husband of the aforementioned blonde saying he will be stopping by this evening with a baseball bat. It's all a matter of where you are and what you're doing that can turn a simple phone call into a bonus or a disaster. This was one of the latter. I was in the middle of working when my cell rang.

Now, when I say I was working, I mean to say I had my foot on a man's throat, slowly crushing his trachea. That's my job. My name is Dakota Bombay, and I'm an assassin. Of course, the damn phone began to ring, and the worst part was that it was playing "Don't Worry, Be Happy."

To be fair, I'd just gotten the phone and hadn't had time to change the ring tone. But how do you scare the hell out of your victim if some stupid shit like that is playing? My victim—or Vic, as we call them in the biz—began to smirk. I scowled and pressed harder with my foot. The son of a bitch was a serial pedophile and the son of a diplomat—meaning he was untouchable to everyone. Everyone, that is, but me.

Damn. The display showed that this was one call I had to take.

"Mom," I said, never losing eye contact with the guy under my shoe. Did I imagine it or did he smirk again? "This is a bad time. I'm working here." I pressed a little harder until I got that oh-so-satisfying gurgle.

"Fine." Mom sniffled and blew her nose into the phone. She was crying. "Call me in five." And with that Carolina Bombay hung up. *Fantastic.*

"Not your lucky day," I said to the vic as I pulled out my silenced Glock .45. "Normally I'd make this look like an accident. But Mom sounds upset, so we need to move this along."

I pulled the trigger twice, and with a *thffft, thffft* it was over. In a few moments I'd retrieved the two spent casings, scanned the area for any evidence I might have left behind, then walked out of the vic's life (or should I say death?).

Mom crying was not a good thing. Not when you come from a family of professional killers. That's right. The Bombay family has been the first name in assassination since 2000 BCE. The legacy is handed down from parent to child, blood relatives only.

Four or five nightmare scenarios went through my mind as I pulled onto the highway and flipped open my phone. It hadn't been a banner year for the Bombays. Just six months ago my sister, Gin, was forced into a messed-up situation by the Council (the family elders who dole out assignments), and her daughter was kidnapped. It all ended up okay. Romi was fine, and Gin was granted an unprecedented early retirement. But after shit like that, you tend to worry a little when your mom's upset.

"Yeah, Mom. What is it?" I'd called her back within five minutes. I'm not a moron. In this family you do what you're told. Discipline comes in the form of an ice pick through the ear instead of the traditional spanking.

I heard a little sniffling and thought that

was weird, because my mom is pretty tough. I mean, she can take on five or six guys and walk away from their corpses without so much as a wrinkle in her denim jumper.

"Romidoesn'twanttocuddleanymore!" she screamed, locked in one long sob and pronouncing the sentence as a single word.

"What?" Maybe I didn't hear her right. Important assassin alert number one: Always know what you heard. One of my great-great-aunts once made a fatal error because she thought she heard, "Kill the Australian prime minister," when what the Council *said* was, "Let's get the Australian prime rib dinner." As a result, Great-great-aunt Orleans was made an example of at the 1965 Bombay family reunion. I guess the old family adage is true: You can't pick your family, but you can pick them off.

Carolina Bombay repeated slowly, "Romi doesn't want to cuddle anymore."

"Uh, and this has *what* to do with me?" I considered asking for Dad to find out if she was going through menopause or toying with insanity. Of course, in this family you couldn't get a section eight to get out of the business. We kind of look at lunacy as a benefit to the job.

"Don't take that tone with me, Dakota Bombay!" *Ah.* The voice was clearer now. "You need to get married and give me more grand-children!"

Okay. She was definitely crazy. And crazy I didn't need. You know how creepy it is when your run-of-the-mill, average parent loses it? Well, it's ten times worse when your mom is one of the best killers in the business.

"Okay, Mom. Calm down. Stop drinking or take some pills or something. 'Cause it won't happen anytime soon."

And that was the truth. I might be thirty-seven, but I was having one hell of a good time. The Bombays lived the good life. Only one or two "assignments" a year, multimillion-dollar trust funds, and performance reviews only every five years. (Those aren't bad. There really is no gray area in "Well, did you kill him or not?") I was too busy jet-setting and sampling the international buffet of leggy blondes to settle down now. Maybe ever.

"Dinner," she said.

"Dinner?" Great, we were down to one-word sentences.

"Yes, dinner tomorrow night at seven." It was amazing (and seriously scary) how quickly her voice went from hysterical to stone-cold professional.

"Um, okay. Why?"

"I'm fixing you up with a nice girl."

"Whoa!" I pulled the car over to the curb,

afraid to drive during this conversation. "No, you're not. Every time you do that it ends in disaster."

"Nonsense." Did Mom actually say *nonsense*? How very Charles Dickens. "It wasn't Millie's fault she had a hump."

I rolled my eyes, wishing she could see me. I continued, "Remember Kelly? She was deathly afraid of trees. Trees! And how about Lacy? She wanted to have eight children and told me I'd be good breeding stock!" I left out Dora, the über-perky Junior Leaguer who dressed like Jackie Onassis and asked if I had any political aspirations (which I thought was ironic). Oh, and Sasha, who passionately loved her job with the Illinois State Museum, where she had devoted her life to studying molds and fungus. (Insert shudder here. She actually said, "You seem like a fun-gi! Get it?" Believe me. I got it.)

"Well, Nora is nothing like those other women. You'll see."

"No, Mom. I'm not coming." I think I even stuck out my lower lip. That's me. The Pouting Assassin. *What?* I am the baby of the family.

"You'll be there if I have to get one of Gin's knockout drugs and tie your unconscious body to one of the dining room chairs."

Okay, she had me there—mainly because my petite, blond mother was strong as an ox run amok on an adrenaline high and as stubborn as a pit bull when you tried to take meat away from it.

"Fine. But no guarantees I'll stay." I made a quick mental note to start carrying a sharp pocketknife with me at all times.

"You'll stay and like it!" With that Mom hung up on me.

So Dakota Bombay, debonair assassin and sophisticated world traveler, was going to Mommy's house tomorrow to meet a girl she hoped I'd marry on the spot, and possibly begin procreating with on the dining room table before dessert.

I did the only thing I could think of: I stopped by my sister's house to complain.

Gin, short for Virginia, is two years older than me. Once widowed with a five-year-old daughter, my big sister is now married to a retired Australian bodyguard.

You might be wondering about all these names: Carolina, Dakota, Virginia. . . . Well, the Bombay family has a lot of weird traditions, including the assigning of geographic names to their progeny. I know—I think it's totally stupid too.

I rang the doorbell and grinned into the security cameras. Bombays are nothing if not security conscious.

"Hey, Dak!" Diego, my brother-in-law from

Down Under, answered the door and ushered me in with a clap on the back.

"Dude," I replied. "How's it going?"

Diego smiled and led me into the kitchen. "Great and quiet. And with your family, that's just the way I like it. Want a beer?" He'd already opened the fridge door and was holding a large can of Foster's lager.

"Yeah." I ran my fingers through my hair. "I just finished a job, and Mom called. So I could use one."

Diego laughed and sat down at the table, handing me a beer while I grabbed some cookies. It still amazed me that he was part of the family now. I mean, Gin's okay, but she's my sister. I don't know how she scored a great guy like this. Especially since she killed his client right out from under him. Oh well, they say opposites attract.

"Uncle Dak!" Romi and Gin burst into the room, and my little niece climbed up onto my lap, fiercely hugging me. Maybe the reason I couldn't commit was that my heart already belonged to this little brat.

"Hey, kid." I squeezed her back. "What's this about you not cuddling with Grandma anymore?"

Gin arched her right eyebrow. "Oh. You heard about that."

"Yeah. Mom called in the middle of my hit,

sobbing that I need to give her more grand-kids. Of course, I blame you."

Gin snatched a bag of Milano cookies from my hands. Sure, they were her cookies, but she could've asked. After all, I was a guest.

"Romi just told Mom she was too old to cuddle all the time," Gin explained.

"Well, thanks to you, I have to have dinner with them and some chick named Nora to-morrow."

Gin and Diego exchanged looks. *Uh-oh.*

"Hey!" I protested. "I saw that. What?"

Gin plucked a cookie out of the bag and pushed the rest to me. *Double uh-oh.*

"Nothing," she said.

Oh, shit. "What? Who is Nora? And why are you looking at me like that?"

Gin shrugged. "She's nice. Pretty, even. And blond. You'd like her."

I rubbed my chin. "Okay. So what's wrong with her?"

Gin looked at Diego, who threw up his hands in protest. She turned back to me. "Well, she's, um, Dad's doctor."

"That doesn't sound so bad." I could do Dad's doctor. As long as she didn't "acciden-tally" screw up his meds when I dumped her.

"What is she? Heart doctor?" Gin shook her head, and I started to sweat. "Podia-trist?" Another no. "Proctologist?" Nope. I had a bad feeling about this. "Chiropractor?" I offered hopefully.

Gin shook her head one more time (and I have to admit I was getting a little sick of that). "She's his . . ." She hesitated for a moment. "ED specialist."

That didn't sound so bad. "What's the ED for?"

The pause got me. I knew I was screwed, because Gin started laughing.

"Erectile dysfunction." Her laughter gained momentum until tears were flowing down her cheeks.

Chapter Two

Lord Melchett: Gray, I suspect, Your Majesty.
Queen Elizabeth: I think you'll find they were orange, Lord Melchett.
Lord Melchett: Gray is more usual, ma'am.
Queen Elizabeth: Who's queen?
Lord Melchett: As you say, Majesty. There were these magnificent orange elephants. . . .
—*Blackadder II*

Usually I sleep in. When you have to kill only one or two people a year, your hours are pretty flexible. I'd say ninety-nine percent of the time I do whatever I want, and one percent is work. It's a damn good ratio. I'm more of a night guy anyway.

Which is why I was pissed off hearing the phone ring at eight o'clock the next morning. This time it was my grandmother.

"Hey, Grandma." I used my most endearing voice, the one that had made her treat me like a sovereign prince all these years. Yes, I'm a spoiled assassin.

"Dakota, dear. How are you?" Grandma Mary replied cheerfully. Normally I'd be nervous about this, but she's been sucking up to me even more lately since she almost had me terminated six months ago. I don't hold a grudge, but I'd be an idiot not to milk it.

"Fine. What's up?" I answered, turning my charm all the way up to eleven.

"Well, the Council has some work for you and Paris. Meet me at the Hyatt in one hour," she ordered.

"The Hyatt? Here in town?" *Grandma's here? Let the spoiling begin!* Last time she showed up she gave me a black American Express card with an unlimited line of credit and a private concierge available twenty-four/seven. I couldn't wait to see what she had for me this time! *What?*

"One hour. I'm calling your cousin now." She hung up.

I jumped out of bed and raced to the shower. Okay, so I had to wait for the blonde in there to finish first. I shoved Jill . . . Jenny . . . Judy (or whatever her name was) out the door, even turning down her offer to spoil me in a different way.

Fifty minutes later I knocked at the presidential suite door, a bouquet of flowers in my hand, ridiculously hyper in anticipation of a spectacular gift.

Paris opened the door. He laughed when he

saw the lilies and ushered me in, showing the ones he'd brought. Grandma gave me a rough kiss and hug and invited us to sit down. I put on my most charming smile and awaited my prize.

"Boys, I called you here because I need your help. The Bombay family business is in trouble."

What? I blinked a few times. The Bombays were in trouble . . . again? And no present?

"Over the years," she continued, ignoring the blatant look of disappointment on my face, "we've grown the business, utilizing the latest technology and intelligence. But that's not working anymore." Her tone changed. "You'd think quality and craftsmanship would be enough these days, but nooooo."

I looked at Paris and he shrugged back at me, presumably pissed about not getting a present too.

"Grandma, what the hell are you talking about?" I asked.

She frowned. "No doubt you thought I was in town to spoil you?"

I stumbled over my denial. "No, ha, ha, ha. Why would you think that?"

Maryland Bombay narrowed her eyes. It was a look she reserved for her victims. "It's time for you two to put your talents to the test for the family. Dakota, with your education in marketing and Paris's MBA from Wharton, I expect great things from you."

Uh-oh. "Grandma," I protested, "I'm not really a marketing consultant. That's just my cover."

Her eyes narrowed to slits. "Did we or did we not send you to Princeton to study marketing? Did you or did you not graduate ranked fifth in your class?"

I ran my fingers through my hair (maybe it wasn't boyishly tousled enough to warrant a present). "Well, sure. But I've kind of been out of practice on that particular skill set. Now, if you want me to kill or seduce someone—that I can do."

She shook her head. "Consider this one of the most important things you can do for the family."

Paris sat there, nodding like a bobble-head dachshund, and I felt a little betrayed that he didn't argue with her too.

I sighed. "When do you need us to start?"

"Now." She smiled as she handed over two large black leather binders. "This is all the activity of the last five fiscals. You'll find our annual reports in there too. I need you both to discover how we can better market our business."

I flipped through the pages of pie charts, organizational flowcharts, and statistics. Which is really weird when you consider that we kill people for money. Who knew the Council was so organized? I blamed the European branch.

"We have annual reports?" I asked. Why did we have annual reports? Who in the hell would we file them with?

"So," Paris interrupted, his eyes never leaving the binder on his lap, "you want branding, focus groups, the whole lot?"

How do you do focus groups for assassination? Find a cross-section of average citizens and ask them, "How do you feel about ice picks versus handguns in life termination?"

"Let me get this straight," I piped up. "You want us to come up with logos and slogans and try them out on random people to find out which sells murder better?"

"Of course not!" Grandma snapped. "The public doesn't know what we do! You're to help the company find our target market!"

Target market? Was she joking?

Paris winked at me, then rolled his eyes to Grandma, indicating he thought I was nuts. *Bastard.*

For a moment I thought I might still be in bed, dreaming. I mean, come *on!* This wasn't the sort of business you created a marketing campaign for. That, and it would be a lot of work. I didn't really have time. There were two new blondes at Gin's spa I hadn't gotten to yet.

Paris looked absorbed. Sure, he loved this stuff. Don't get me wrong—he's my wingman—but why would he take this seriously?

"Um, Grandma?" I hesitated. "Why would slogans and logos help us? Aren't our main clients various government agencies? They don't care about this crap. They just want re-sults." And unless I was totally off base here, *results* meant lifeless corpses—not a list of goals, objectives, and action items.

Grandma leaned back with a sigh. "Well, we aren't getting as much work as we used to."

Paris spoke up (finally!). "So, the Council thinks a jazzed-up image will tell the CIA we are ready to take on more assignments?"

"Actually, boys, we just need to prove that like every other family business, we can adapt—change with progress."

"Why don't we just get out of the business entirely?" To be fair, this was a valid question. Our individual trust funds (from four millen-nia of wet work) each exceeded $100 million.

"Dammit, Dak!" Grandma sputtered, her face turning an alarming shade of mauve. "Get with the program! This is what Bom-bays do! It's what we've always done! Why should we stop now when we're the best in the business?"

Paris looked at me, then turned to her. "Maybe Dak is right, though." I mentally made a note to cancel that body check I had been planning to give him in the hallway when we were done. "We've owned the assassination market for centuries. Why not quit while we're ahead?"

I nodded in agreement, but it felt as if I were in the movie *Jackass* and had just agreed to do something that would involve my testicles, jumper cables, and a rusty WWII battery.

She shook her head. "Just because Gin has retired doesn't mean you can too. No. This is our family's honor we're talking about." She stood, indicating that we should leave. "You have two weeks before you make your presentation to the Council. I'll have Missi set up the multimedia equipment in the auditorium at Santa Muerta. I'll expect at least Power-Point 2007 for the presentation." She herded us to the door and opened it. "That's all. I want to see some real outside-the-box thinking from you two."

As the door shut on my stunned face, I couldn't help wondering if the box she was referring to was my coffin.

Chapter Three

"What do you get when you cross a cataclysm with a hellhole? A catastrofuck."
                —Jon Stewart, *The Daily Show*

I don't know which freaked me out more: the new job, Dad seeing an erectile-dysfunction specialist, or Mom setting me up with his doctor. To tell the truth I was a bit insulted. Did my family think I was dating a steady stream of blondes because I had a . . . um, problem? Or was this just sport for them?

I stomped around my condo for an hour, slamming doors and throwing a tantrum no one would see. *For Christ's sake!* I had no problem getting it up. All my guns were fully loaded! I didn't shoot blanks! I didn't run out of ammo at the wrong time either!

Okay, this is not a big deal. I'll just go over to Mom's, sit through dinner calmly, then make my excuses and leave.

Another thought occurred to me: Maybe I

should bag Nora. Prove to her I didn't have a problem. That would solve it. I could wear that woman out with one of my all-night erections. That would show her. And when she called Mom the next day and said she was too exhausted to date me, my family would know too.

That sounded like a good plan. I spent more time getting ready than I ever had for a date before. From my perfectly tousled hair to the tips of my Bruno Magli loafers, I was ready. I just had to pick up an expensive bottle of wine and head to my parents' house, and later I would make Nora see God.

The bottle of Bordeaux was expensive. I used the AmEx black card—that would show Grandma for not giving me a present. I pulled into my parents' place and noticed the Lexus in the driveway. Promising. At least this Nora had her own money. I guess the hard cash is in soft dicks these days. Then I remembered that Dad was funding that Lexus and shuddered again.

"Hey, Mom." I hugged her warmly as she ushered me in the house, and I handed the bottle of wine to Dad. He rolled his eyes, and we had a father-son moment of silent communication.

"And this," Mom said casually, "is Nora Adams."

I unleashed my best smile. "It's nice to meet you." I shook her hand. She was blond and cute, like Gin said. Short, curly hair, blue eyes, and a decent smile. Not totally my type, but I could do her.

"Thanks," she said. "It's nice to meet you too."

Oh . . . my . . . God. She had a man voice. Not a smoky Kathleen Turner voice or a sultry Demi Moore voice, but a deep, unabashed man voice. A thought terrified me: Maybe she was a man.

Mom pushed us toward the dining room, and I held out Nora's chair for her. I sat opposite Dad, between Nora and Mom.

"So, Dakota," Nora's bass boomed, "your mom tells me you're a consultant?"

I struggled to clear my head. I was really freaked out by her voice. "Um, yeah. I'm a marketing consultant."

At this point it was usually customary to ask her what she did, but I really didn't want to hear the details. I knew more than enough already. So I asked her where she was from, that kind of thing. As she droned on in a voice that would make a Green Beret feel girlie, I caught Mom's expression out of the corner of my eye. She was staring at me. I tried to ignore it, but I couldn't. My sweet and petite mother resembled a cobra trying to hypnotize its prey. Hey, no pressure here, right?

"And after that I did a stint with the merchant marines in 'ninety-two," Nora said, and I forced myself to focus. So, I did the mature thing: I stuck out my tongue at Mom and turned to Nora.

"That sounds fascinating. Wow. You surf, participate in triathlons, ride rodeo, and whittle. Where do you find time for a social life?" I tried my best to be charming, but at this point I was convinced she actually was a man. At least deep down inside.

Dinner was awkward. Very, very awkward. But I managed to charm a few boyish smiles out of Nora. I thanked my mom for dinner, winked at Dad, and took Nora home to prove to her and everyone that I, Dakota Bombay, had no trouble in bed.

All night long I made merciless, passionate love to this woman, pleasing her in ways she never imagined. She had more than twenty orgasms, and finally, at four thirty a.m., she begged me to stop and called me the greatest lover she'd ever been with. She was even considering writing an article about me for the *Journal of the American Medical Association.*

Well, at least, that was how I imagined it would go. If the truth must be told (and if this gets out to anyone in my family, I will hunt you down and kill you), it was a major disaster.

I'm going to say it was the man voice, the man hobbies, and the horrible pressure of trying to succeed under all the above circumstances. I refuse to believe I have a problem.

That's right: I couldn't get it up. Laugh if you want to, but I can kill anyone with nothing more than a pair of tweezers, so you make that choice.

We started making out, you know, the usual. I turned the lights out initially, but her voice was such a turnoff I turned them back on, because in the dark she seemed too masculine. Nora wasn't a bad kisser, and we moved on to fondling. That seemed to help, except that I just couldn't get hard. I figured all I had to do was get her clothes off. The sight of a naked woman always worked.

Then I saw the tattoos. What kind of woman has an anchor with the word *Mom* written on it? I swear, my dick actually receded into my body in revolt. The final insult? She handed me her card as she got dressed and left. Nora thought I'd benefit from an appointment.

I showered for a long, long time. I even gargled for a full thirty seconds with Listerine. (The new whitening kind, of course. I use every opportunity to work on my smile.) Even though I knew Nora was a woman, it still grossed me out.

As I lay on my bed, I began to lecture my penis. "You're my go-to guy! How could you let this happen? You're immune to this shit!" That kind of stuff. I don't know if other men yell at their penis, but I felt it had let me down, and therefore should be punished.

Publicity Network was a group I'd joined after college, made up of local public relations and marketing professionals. I thought it would be a great way to work my cover and pick up women. I was right on both counts.

The meetings took place once a month at a local hotel and featured lunch, a speaker, and networking opportunities. Ironically, the next day was one of those meetings.

As I stood in line, wearing my khakis, blue shirt, and tie with navy blazer, of course, I scanned the room. The trick was to make people think I worked as a consultant in their field. They had to believe I was committed to a life of telling people how great some eczema cream was, or why they should invest in their children's education at a prep school. Actually, it wasn't very hard. PR is mainly bullshit, and I was the king.

"Bernie!" I sat down with my plate full of

food and thumped the one guy I did like on the back. He was the director of communications for the Boy Scouts and a really funny dude.

"Dakota! Good to see you! Have you met everyone?" He motioned around the table of all men. I nodded through the introductions. Some of them I'd met before—some were new. I didn't really care. Maybe I'd glean something useful to take to Paris that afternoon.

Bernie and I chatted for a little while. He told me a funny story about a crisis involving a leader who recently had his Boy Scouts use poison ivy for toilet paper. I could've listened to him all day, but we were interrupted.

"May I join you?" asked a tall woman with flaming red hair. She looked annoyed more than anything, and I watched as the other men at the table tried to figure out what they should do. They reminded me of lemmings on the edge of a cliff.

Bernie pointed at the only open chair. "Please."

The woman turned to face me. For some reason I was a little stunned. Tall and thin, she had long, curly red hair, light blue eyes, pale skin, and freckles. Her features were elfin, with large eyes, a little upturned nose, and a Cupid's-bow mouth. I was so startled I didn't know what to say next. Then I realized she was speaking.

"No other open seats," she said as she placed her napkin on her lap.

"No problem." Bernie smiled. He was the only one behaving like an adult. "My name's Bernie Paulson. I work for the Boy Scouts. And this is Dakota Bombay. He's a consultant." He then went on to introduce the other stunned men at the table.

"Nice to meet you. I'm Leonie Doubtfire."

"Seriously?" I asked before thinking (one of my less endearing traits).

Leonie looked right into my eyes, as if she were daring me to say something stupid. Something about those eyes made me start to sweat—and I never do that. No woman had ever made me nervous before. But this one was fascinating. I found myself admiring her fearlessness. In fact, I'm pretty sure I admired her throughout the presentation.

The lecture was "Finding Your Brand," but I had a hard time keeping up with it. For some reason I was completely focused on Ms. Doubtfire. I tried not to stare, but it was impossible.

Forcing my eyes away, I scanned the room. There were other women there—many blondes. I'd slept with a number of them. Of course, I would never work with them. Never bag a client—that's what I would say if I ever had clients, which I didn't.

Before I knew it the lunch had concluded. Again I tore my eyes away from Leonie to pretend I'd been paying attention. People were starting to get up and mingle before heading back to work. When I looked across the table the redhead was gone.

"Good to see you again, Dak." Bernie shook my hand.

"Where did she go?" I fumbled.

He smiled. "She probably thought you were stalking her, the way you kept staring at her like that."

I winced, realizing he was right. I had been staring. And for some strange reason I felt a little depressed that she was gone. I looked at the chair she sat in and spotted a small compact. Picking it up, I realized that Cinderella had left something at the ball. If I ever saw her again I'd be able to return it. Of course, then she'd really think I was creepy.

I said my good-byes and left, circling the parking lot twice to see if I could spot her. Shaking my head to clear it, I headed to Paris's place. And then I remembered last night, and all thoughts of Leonie Doubtfire vanished.

"You're impotent?" Paris's eyes grew wide with amazement.

I shushed him and looked around—a weird thing, because we were in his apartment. Still, six months ago Gin had bugged my and Paris's phone lines, so I didn't put it past the family to have their ears and eyes on us at all times.

"No!" I shouted a little too forcefully. "No. I couldn't help it. She sounded like a man. And Mom was staring at me all through dinner. There was too much pressure to perform!"

Paris shook his head. "I don't know, man. You've never had a problem like this before."

"I know! It's making me crazy! What do I do?"

Paris looked around his apartment, as if the answer would automatically materialize in the blender, lamp shade, or ceiling fan. He had a great place. Paris was an artistic sort. I'd recently found out he wrote poetry. The apartment was filled with artwork—paintings, sculptures, and architecturally designed furniture. I used to think he had one hell of an interior designer, but after the poetry revelation I figured he did it himself.

"You have to sleep with the other women your mom set you up with," he announced, looking pleased with himself.

"What?" My mind turned back to Dora and Millie. I shuddered again and realized I was doing that a lot. "Why can't I just spend the weekend in the arms of a couple of Swedish twins?" That seemed more reasonable to me. And I could find 'em too. Some people have "gaydar." Some people have "beerdar." I had "blondar."

"No. You have to prove that you can screw anyone. Not just your type." He paused, rubbing his chin. "Maybe blondes have ruined you. Maybe you can't have sex with any woman who goes against your type."

"That's the stupidest thing I ever heard. I can do any woman. Hair color and legginess don't matter." They didn't. *Right?*

"What about that Kelly girl?" Paris asked.

"The one who's afraid of trees?" *Hmmm.* Theoretically there was nothing physically wrong with her. She was actually cute. A brunette, but cute. I'd just have to keep her in the bedroom and remove the bamboo plant in the corner, but I could do that.

"Okay. I'll give her a call." I picked up my cell phone and dialed.

You might think it's strange that I had her number, but I had every woman's number in my cell phone. Mom would text them to me and I'd enter them before meeting them. I've never erased a single one. But I did code them. For example, Dora's number came up with a photo of Lee Harvey Oswald. Millie's had Quasimodo. That kind of thing. *What?*

Chapter Four

"I would like, if I may, to take you on a strange journey."
—The Criminologist, *The Rocky Horror Picture Show*

After Kelly agreed (a bit too eagerly) to my suggestion of dinner the next night, Paris and I got to work on the marketing plans for the Bombay family business.

"Man, I can't believe we did work for the Republicans four times this century." Paris shook his head. "Although that kind of makes sense, now that I think of it."

I leafed through a few pages of my binder. "I can't believe the family actually wrote this shit down! I mean, look at this one!" I pointed at the high-profile hit of a politician in the nineteenth century. I'd tell you more, but I had to sign a confidentiality clause in my own blood when I was five. You might think we'd forget something that happened when we were little, but there's something about a family blood ritual and Grandma in a goat-skull headdress that sticks in your mind.

Paris nodded. "Yeah. Well, at least we have a record of who our main clients are."

"Are you even surprised? I mean, we always suspected the CIA, the Feds, Interpol, and the Yard, and here it is in black and white." And color too. Grandma did the pie charts as literal cherry pies, and all the bullet points were little skulls.

"Okay," Paris said, "where do we start?"

"I wonder if it's hereditary," I mused aloud.

"What?" Paris cocked his right eyebrow. *Bastard.* I've never been able to do that.

"You know. ED. I mean, Dad has it, right?"

Paris stared at me. "Will you give it up and concentrate? This presentation is important!"

I sat back in my chair. "And you're just eating it up, right?"

"What the hell are you talking about?" Paris growled.

I stabbed my finger at him. "You love doing this. You've probably been waiting your whole life for this type of assignment."

He slapped my hand away. "Oh, for Christ's sake. You're pissed because I didn't argue with Grandma about it."

Damn. He nailed it. I never could get away with anything where Paris, his sister Liv, or Gin was concerned. And you can bet one of my dazzling smiles wasn't going to get me out of this one.

"Fine." I was behaving like an immature jerk, but losing access to your favorite appendage will do that to a man. "Let's get this over with."

We spent the afternoon going through the binders, ass-deep in reports on the financial history of the Bombay clan's greatest hits. And I'll grudgingly admit it was kind of fascinating. I was pretty sure no one but the Council had access to the history of a family of assassins spanning four thousand years. You couldn't find this stuff on genealogy.com.

"All right." I leaned back in my chair and pushed the binder to the middle of the table. "I'm done for today." I looked at my TAG Heuer watch. "Got a hot date tonight with a tree hater."

Paris and I agreed to meet up again tomorrow, but from the look on his face he was going to keep working. *Bastard.* He'd probably get the bigger gift from Grandma too.

Back at home I stashed the bamboo plant and anything with a tree motif in the shed. I had to succeed tonight. My next dilemma was more difficult. It took me two hours, but I finally managed to find a restaurant with no trees outside or in. I didn't realize how hard it would be. After finding a route with the fewest trees from Kelly's house to the Flaming Lemur, I jumped in the shower and got ready.

Kelly answered her door with a big smile and a little black dress. We drove to the restaurant with no incident and even made it to our table without a freakout.

"I'm so glad you called, Dakota," she purred. "I was afraid you'd forgotten about me."

"Impossible." How did you forget about a woman who couldn't even go outside? "I've been looking forward to this." Not a lie! Of course, I was more looking forward to nailing her than talking to her, but first things first.

She took her napkin and placed it on her lap. "I suppose you're wondering if I'm still dendrophobic?"

It has a name? "Are you?" I asked.

"No. I have a great therapist. Actually, my fear of trees was related to a fear of sex." Before I could stop it I immediately pictured a forest full of erections.

"Did you conquer that fear?" I asked, hoping my desperation wasn't obvious in my voice.

"Yes, I did." She grinned wickedly and it was way cute. "In fact, I'm not afraid of sex anymore either."

I lifted my glass of wine. "Well, then we have something to celebrate." The glasses clinked and I watched as she drank, her gaze never leaving mine. The air was thick with sexual tension, just the way I liked it. This was going to be a breeze.

It was obvious that small talk wasn't her thing. Kelly mainly leered at me through dinner, her foot sliding up and down my shin. Oh, she was up for it. I was gonna get laid tonight and prove it was just Nora's masculinity that distracted me.

In fact, this chick was all over me while I drove home. Kelly kept kissing my neck, her hands on my groin the whole way. I guess I might have misjudged her. My tree was getting harder by the minute. *Yay!*

The door barely closed before she'd flung me against the closet, grinding her hips into mine, crushing my lips with hers. I did the only thing I could do: I carried her into my bedroom.

I unzipped her dress with great expectation and slid it to the floor. She was so hot and ready I thought I would burst.

"Hold on," Kelly said, pushing me back. "I need to freshen up first." She blew me a kiss; then in her adorable bra and panties she took her purse into the bathroom.

I don't think I've ever gotten undressed faster in my life. I experimented with different lounging positions on the bed, keeping on my black silk boxer shorts. I was ready . . .

beyond ready. I warned my dick not to fail me now as the bathroom door opened.

I can't blame my dick for this one. Really. It went from hard to soft in a split second as Kelly stood in front of me. I was more terrified than anything.

Apparently she had lost her fear of trees by channeling another neurosis. There she was, dressed in a diaper and a baby bonnet, with a pacifier in her mouth.

"What the hell?" I asked.

"Baby wants Dak," Kelly pulled the pacifier from her lips and responded in a childlike voice. "Change baby!" she demanded, tossing me a bottle of baby powder.

"What?"

"Change baby and powder baby's butt!" she roared.

I'd heard about infantilism. I'm not sheltered. I know there are people who get off on this. Hell, one of Gin's college roommates wore footie jammies and carried a blankie. But I didn't have sex with her.

"*Change baby!*" Kelly shrieked. Then she went into a full toddler temper tantrum. I kid you not.

I watched in horror for five minutes, then handed back her dress. There would be no erection tonight. "It's past baby's bedtime."

Kelly glared at me, then took the dress and

ran into the bathroom, slamming the door. I waited in the hall, car keys in hand, and tried to burn the image of what I'd just seen out of my mind.

"It's completely healthy, you know!" Kelly lectured me all the way home, telling me about a group she belonged to where they got together at a pretend day care center, slept in cribs, and got changed by large German nannies. It didn't matter. As I dropped her off at her house I deleted her name and number from my cell phone—a first for me. I shuddered all the way home and showered for an hour.

Just before I fell asleep I wondered if this was a setup by the Bombays. Maybe they were developing some new "erection assassination" program. For once I felt as if there were something worse than death.

Chapter Five

"And now for something completely different . . ."
—Announcer, *Monty Python's Flying Circus*

The next morning I was having this dream where all the blondes in the world were trying to change my diaper when the doorbell rang.

I thought about letting it go. But then I remembered that I was meeting Paris and shrugged on pajamas and a bathrobe and answered the door.

"Dakota Bombay?" asked a tall, thin man in a cheap suit. *Damn.* I should have checked the security monitors. I was getting too sloppy.

Oh, well. Maybe he'd put me out of my misery. We always lived with the fear of being offed by the competition. So be it. Death would be welcome.

I sighed. "Yes."

The man extended his hand. "Bob Riley from Child Welfare Services."

Oh, shit! Had Kelly called this guy for abuse of a minor? It sounded twisted, but my brain was outpacing rationality.

I shook his hand. That was when I noticed he wasn't alone. Standing next to Bob Riley was a little blond kid with enormous blue eyes, staring at me.

"May we come in, Mr. Bombay?" Bob asked, and I ushered them into the living room.

"What's this about?" I demanded. I couldn't take my eyes off the kid, who suddenly grinned, revealing a crooked smile and a gap between his two front teeth.

"I realize this may come as something of a shock, Mr. Bombay, but this is your son. Louis."

That was when I knew there was a conspiracy against me. "What . . . what did you say?" I gasped.

Bob frowned as if he disapproved of my response. "This is your son. His mother"— he looked at his clipboard—"Helga Torvald, died a month ago. In her will she stipulated that her son live with his biological father. That's you."

My jaw hurt from being locked in an open expression. "My son? I don't have any children. There must be some mistake!" I looked at the kid and watched his smile vanish. *Damn.* I wished I hadn't said that. It wasn't this kid's fault.

"I'm afraid not, Mr. Bombay." Bob handed me some paperwork that listed me as the father of Louis Torvald. There were photos of me and Helga together in a hot tub. She looked just like all of the other women I'd dated.

Bob Riley stood up and took back the clipboard. "Here is my number. Call me if you have any questions." He turned and headed toward the door.

I raced after him. "Wait! You can't just leave this kid here."

Bob turned to face me, and I toyed with killing him. "His name is Louis, Mr. Bombay. And he's your son. Where else would I leave him?" He was gone before I could respond.

I stared at the door for quite a while, trying to absorb this information. It couldn't be true! The kid was, like, five or six! Why didn't this Helga tell me I'd fathered a child?

Then it hit me. It was a joke! Gin knew Mom was giving me a hard time about having kids. She'd obviously set this up! I gave Louis some cookies (what kid doesn't love cookies? *I* love cookies) and called Gin, Liv, and Paris, telling them to come over immediately. I was dressed before the doorbell rang.

My sister and two cousins arrived at the

exact same time—proof that they were all in on this. I led them to the dining room where Louis was sitting at the table, his legs dangling a foot or so off the ground. He looked up with a smile. I knew it!

"Aha!" I proclaimed, pointing at the boy. Actually, I was pretty proud of the fact that I'd figured it out. It was a very good joke.

"Aha what?" Gin asked, eyes bulging as she took in the kid. "Who's this?"

Liv clapped her hands together. "He's adorable! Are you babysitting?" Ever the maternal type, she ran over and hugged Louis.

Paris eyed me suspiciously. "Man, you went to a lot of trouble to get out of working today. I never thought you'd pull something like this."

"What?" My triumphant face fell. "It's a joke, right? You set me up with that Bob Riley from Child Services, and Louis." *Right?*

"Dak." Gin stared at me blankly. "What are you talking about?"

I looked around the table and knew I was screwed. It wasn't a joke. *Shit.*

Gin called Mom and Dad, and there I was, explaining to the whole family about my new son, Louis. Who, by the way, hadn't said a word the whole time.

Mom ran over and gathered the boy in her arms. Louis snuggled against her with a shy grin.

"I can't believe this!" Gin sounded angry. "You are so irresponsible!"

"He's absolutely wonderful!" Liv said, eyes shining.

Mom piped up, "He looks just like you did when you were . . . um, how old is Louis?"

Paris glared at me, presumably pissed because we weren't going to work on his beloved project for the Council today. Dad gave me the thumbs-up. Of course, then I remembered that his thumbs were the only thing on him going up lately. I shuddered.

"Louis," I said, crouching in front of him, "Grandma asked how old you are."

The boy looked at me for a moment, then turned to Mom and threw his arms around her neck. He still hadn't said a word, but Mom was in heaven.

"So," Gin asked, "what are you going to do?"

I ran my hands through my hair. What was I going to do? "I have no idea."

"I'd say he's about Romi and Alta's age," she said quietly. "You'll have to enroll him in their school so they can show him around."

"And don't forget to add him to your insurance," Liv added.

"You'll need a sitter for this afternoon," Paris growled, still obviously fixated on work.

Dad just sat there and grinned. *Thanks, Dad.*

"You'll need to turn the guest room into his room," Mom said in a love-struck voice. "And we'll have to go shopping for clothes and toys!" Clearly I was now off the hook with her in the grandkid department. Somehow that didn't make me feel better.

"Hold on!" I brought my hands up in front of me to fend off the maternal brigade. "I don't know what I'm going to do yet."

"Do?" Mom glared at me. "What do you mean? He's your son, Dak! You have to take care of him. Raise him!"

"And since he's yours by blood," Paris interrupted, "you'll have to start training him."

Gin would have said something if she weren't on the phone telling Diego to bring Romi over immediately to meet her new cousin.

The whole room erupted in discussion. I stumbled backward, falling into a chair and slumping in defeat. We hadn't even determined paternity, and everyone assumed Louis was part of the family.

I had to give it to the kid: He really glowed with all the praise and adoration. But he still hadn't said anything. What was up with that? Plus, I realized that having a new son would put a serious crimp in my mission to prove my manhood.

My head hurt. Between the run of bad-women luck, the crazy assignment from the Council, and the appearance of my "son," I was pretty sure one of the arteries throbbing in my forehead would burst. Maybe I should get Gin and Diego to agree to be his guardians once I died from this.

"Well, I think that went rather well." A small voice seemed to emanate from my alleged son once everyone had left. I peeked cautiously through my fingers.

"Excuse me?" I asked, mouth agape (which, by the way, is not a good look for me).

Louis came over and sat at the table next to me, his chin resting in his hand. "I'm not saying it was perfect, but it was good. My new family is very nice."

I stared at him. The damn kid hadn't uttered a word the whole time! Now he sounded like . . . like an old Jewish comedian working in the Catskills.

"'Sup, Sheckie? Why are you talking now?" I asked.

The so-called fruit of my loins responded, "Sheckie? Come on, Dad. I can barely stand Louis. Mom thought it sounded intelligent."

"How old are you?" I asked. Maybe he was a midget teenager. Then I wouldn't need a sitter.

Louis rolled his eyes. "Not very good at this, are you? I'm six."

"You're shitting me!" I said before I could stop myself.

Louis frowned. "You're not supposed to use that kind of language around me." He looked around the room. "Actually, this place seems more like a bachelor pad than a home for a kid."

He was right. I didn't know what to do. This kid was freaking me out.

"So, what are the schools like here?" Louis continued. "Mom moved around a lot, so I've been exposed to several different curricula."

I searched my mind for info on his mother. I didn't think I'd ever dated anyone as smart as this kid. Where did the brains come from?

"Romi seems nice. Although a little young. I'm used to older companions."

Companions? What kind of six-year-old referred to other kids as companions? I rolled my eyes. "Used to spending time with physicists and philosophers, are you?"

Then Louis did something that made my heart sink. He narrowed his eyes and frowned. I'd seen that expression all my life on my grandmother's, mother's, and sister's faces. *My God.* He really was my son. The realization was too much. All the blood that should have been flowing to my cock (*hear that, you stupid prick?*) drained to my feet. Which was how I ended up in a clump on the floor.

Chapter Six

"Blinded by the light. Remmed up like a do-
cent in the humble of the might."

—Paul, *The Vacant Lot*

Mom and Gin showed up later that night with
shopping bags full of clothes, toys, and more
presents than I had ever gotten. Of course,
they were for Louis. While Mom bathed him
and tucked him into my old guest room, Gin
lectured me on what I needed to do to register
him for school the next day.

"You should get to Kennedy Elementary
early so they can show you around and he
can sit in on a class." Gin was focused. This
was her thing. Gin was even in the PTA.

"I don't know. I was thinking of taking him
to the hospital."

My sister looked alarmed. "Why? Is he sick?"

"No. I just thought I'd get a head start on
the paternity test."

Gin frowned and narrowed her eyes—just

45

like Louis had. They could be mother and son. I gulped.

"Dak! That boy is your son. His mother just died. If you run him in for the tests tomorrow, he'll think you don't want him."

"I don't want him!" I cried.

Gin responded with a right cross to my jaw. She was good. That was going to leave a mark.

She crossed her arms over her chest. *Uh-oh.* "You, little brother, are going to grow up, once and for all. You were stupid enough to ignore birth control, and now you're gonna be a man or I will kill you." I was pretty sure she meant it.

"What's all the yelling out here?" Mom came out of my guest . . . um, Louis's room, that same Louisy scowl on her face. "I just got him to sleep. What is wrong with you two?"

Gin threw her arms up in the air and dropped into a chair. I thought that looked like a good idea, so I sat on the couch.

"I think you'd better stay the night, Mom." I was pretty sure she'd turn me down. But I was way over my head here.

"Of course," she responded. Apparently I'd underestimated her maternal instincts. I gave her a dazzling smile.

"Don't pull that shit with me, Dakota." She sighed. "I'm doing this because I'm afraid if I don't, you'll sneak off to the bars tonight, leaving my grandson alone."

She can read minds? You know, that explains so much.

"Well, thanks for that vote of confidence," I responded.

"So. You're a father now," Gin said. "What are you going to do to take care of my nephew?"

I looked at the two most important women in my life. Mom, who coddled and spoiled me. Gin, who taught me how to sight a sniper rifle and used to beat up my bullies. And who very recently saved my life. *Damn.* I was totally screwed.

"I'll take him to school tomorrow. Then, this weekend, I'll find something for us to do together. Get to know him, that kind of thing." I sounded mature, but really I was just saying what I thought they wanted to hear.

"I think this will be good for you, Dak," Gin said as she picked up her jacket from the back of the couch. "Maybe you'll grow up." She kissed Mom on the cheek and made it out the door before I could say something cutting and witty. I don't know what that would have been, but if I had something, I would've said it.

Mom brought her duffel bag in from the car and in minutes had changed into jammies. She took my room (it was closer to Louis), and I had the couch.

I'd bought the sofa for its make-outability. I've never had to sleep on it. Oh, well. I had a son now. It was time to make sacrifices. As I lay there, uncomfortable as hell, I thought that at least I'd given Mom what she wanted. Maybe she'd back off on the whole notion of me getting married. Maybe it wouldn't be so bad after all. I got the kid without the work.

"When are you going to give Louis a mother?"

I woke up to find Carolina Bombay standing over me. I looked at the clock: three forty-five a.m.

"Jeez, Mom! Go to bed!" I was pissed. I'd been in the middle of a dream where I was being bathed by naked Nordic women. And they were giggling. A lot.

Mom sighed her eternal sigh of martyrdom (after almost forty years, she really had it down) and padded off to my room. Fortunately I was able to pick up the dream again. Unfortunately we'd apparently gotten past the sex and were all fully clothed. *Thanks, Mom.*

I got up a few hours later and sat in the kitchen with a cup of black coffee. It was way too early for Louis or Mom to be up, but I couldn't sleep.

My masculinity was in serious trouble, and I knew it. In the last few days I'd had erectile dysfunction twice, fainted, and gotten socked on the jaw by my sister and bullied by Mom. My life was completely messed up, and I didn't have anyone I could kill . . . I mean blame. Now all I had was no sex life, actual marketing work for the family, and a son. What the hell?

It was obvious that Gin wouldn't take Louis and raise him. She'd been my best shot. Maybe Mom would, but then, she would've taken him home last night. I walked down the hall to my guest . . . I mean son's room. The walls were covered with airplanes, trains, and cars. How in the hell did they wallpaper that room without my knowing? That was creepy.

My eyes rested on Louis. He looked pretty cute all curled up and sleeping. I know this will sound weird, but I do love kids. Romi has me wrapped around her cute little finger. I just thought I had more time for fatherhood. And I kind of expected a kid who talked like a kid, not Einstein.

Louis sighed and rolled over. He looked so small. I remembered that he was here because his mom was dead. The guilt hit me harder than Gin's right cross. This little kid was holding up well, especially being with the dad he'd never known. I should cut him some slack. He wasn't really responsible for my problems.

I didn't know how long I stood there watching him, but it must have been a while, because the doorbell rang. The Thomas the Tank Engine clock said seven a.m.

Gin and Romi pushed past me through the doorway and raced off to Louis's room. Obviously they both thought I was completely useless. I followed them to find Mom fully dressed (how the hell did she do that in the time it took me to answer the door?), with Gin choosing Louis's clothes. Louis and Romi were in the kitchen having cereal for breakfast. I must move in slow motion, I thought to myself. Either that or I was experiencing a blackout. How did these women move so damned fast?

So, being totally ignored, I showered and dressed. At eight a.m. we rolled out like some Secret Service caravan—Gin's black minivan, my black SUV, and Mom's black Town Car. In minutes we pulled up in front of Kennedy Elementary.

"Here are some forms that need to be filled out by the parent," Mrs. White, the secretary, informed me. Mr. Steuland took Louis down to his new classroom. Gin had just returned from dropping Romi at her class, and Mom stared at me as if she thought I was about to sprout two new heads.

I turned toward the paperwork. How hard could this be? Full name. *Um.* Louis Torvald-Bombay. Middle name? *Shit.* Tripped up by the second question. That couldn't be good. I looked up at Gin and Mom, but they wouldn't know either. I'd just skip that. Address—no problem. Parents' information—easy. Date of birth. *Uh-oh.* I could just make that up, I guessed. But that would make me look stupid when Louis corrected me (and I was pretty sure he would).

I tried to skip some, but the questions just got harder. Social Security number? Kids had those? I hadn't gotten one until I turned twelve. Physical ailments? Should I put overdeveloped brain? Medical history and shots? Dental exam? I was so screwed.

"Um"—I looked up at Mrs. White—"can I take this home with me and bring it back?" Mom and Gin looked at each other as if they knew I couldn't do it.

"Certainly, Mr. Bombay." Mrs. White smiled. "Your sister explained the situation. I imagine you have paperwork on your son at home. Just bring it in tomorrow morning."

Gin scolded me on the way out to the car. "You don't know his birthday?" She stopped walking and looked back at the school. "They aren't supposed to let him attend school without a physical."

I was getting sick of her. "Don't go back there and tell them that! I have five hours to myself today, and I need it."

She turned toward me. "This is not all about you!"

"Just shut up, Gin!" *Oooh.* Oscar Wilde I ain't.

"I could just kill you for being so irresponsible!" she yelled.

"I should kill you just for hitting me yesterday!" I shouted back.

"Knock it off or I'll kill both of you," Mom hissed. That worked—mainly because we knew she could. And she'd make it hurt, too. There was no quarter given where Mom was concerned.

The three of us stormed off to our cars, agreeing to meet back at the school at three p.m. I went home and called that pencil neck who dropped off my son, wondering if the Council would allow me to kill him for not telling me my son's middle name. *Priorities*, I told myself. *Get the paperwork first— kill him later.*

Chapter Seven

"Have you ever tried to pick up your teeth with broken fingers?"
— Fergus, *The Crying Game*

The next thirty-six hours (that's how assassins think—in hours, not days) were a blur. Bob Riley apologized profusely for not giving me the paperwork.

I had to give Helga credit: She'd kept medical records from the day Louis was born. He didn't have a middle name, though. How weird was that?

Louis and I settled into a sort of routine. I took him to school and picked him up afterward. We'd chat about nothing—mostly because I couldn't understand a word he said—get through dinner at a fast-food restaurant; then it would be bedtime and we'd do it all over again.

I think the kid and I were warming up to

each other. But I hadn't had sex in a week, and that was a serious dry spell for me.

Since I couldn't do much about the sex with Louis around, I agreed to meet Paris after dropping Junior off at school the next day.

"This is due in eight days," Paris said.

I sighed. "I know. So let's get to it."

"Tomorrow's Saturday. Liv says you're spending the weekend with Louis." He scowled.

I slapped the table. "Listen! Do you want to do this or not? My life hasn't exactly been a bunch of roses lately! Cut me some slack or do it yourself!"

Paris leaned back. "All right. I get it. Sorry I've been pushing it. I know you've had a lot on your mind, with the kid and celibacy and all. Let's talk about it now and get it over with."

I shook my head. "Let's not. It's all I've been thinking about for the last four days. I'd rather be distracted by this crap."

Paris studied me for a moment, then nodded. He'd been my best friend since we were little kids. Hell, we'd even trained together. So he knew when to give up.

"All right," he said. "I've gone over this stuff and noticed that in the last two years our assignments have decreased by twenty-five percent."

I tapped my pencil. "Maybe there are fewer

people to kill? Maybe they don't have as many assignments to hand out anymore?"

"No, I don't think so. Look at these figures." He pushed his laptop toward me. "Our workload has been steady for four thousand years. This is the first time we've had a dropoff."

"Okay. So you think we need to work on our image?"

Paris nodded. "I've come up with some ideas. Nowadays companies use branding to reinforce their status with consumers. I've been working on some logos." He slid the laptop toward me again.

"Jesus, Paris!" The screen was filled with every image of death you could imagine, but with a Madison Avenue–type spin. There were skulls, coffins, and nooses superimposed over staplers, file folders, and computers (staplers?). "I don't know about this."

"Okay." Paris pushed another key on the laptop. "How about this?"

You might think that as an assassin I'd seen everything. And up until that moment I would have agreed with you. But we'd both be wrong. Dead wrong.

There on the screen, in full color, was Grandma, dressed like the Orkin Man, holding an Uzi instead of bug spray or whatever the hell it is that they hold. She was smiling, standing next to the legs and feet of an apparently dead man. The caption read: *Bombay Pest Exterminators—Discreet and Efficient Disposal of Your Problems Since 2000 BCE.*

"Are you shitting me?" I asked Paris. Maybe he was.

A hurt look crossed his face. "No. This is what I came up with."

"Jesus, Par! You can't do that."

Paris threw his pen at the table. "Well, if you'd been here to help me, I could've come up with something better!"

"If you think for one minute I'd rather have a dick malfunction, dating problems, and a new son, you're more screwed up than I thought you were!" I shouted.

Paris sank his face into his hands. "Shit," was all he said.

I took a few minutes to calm down. This wasn't his fault. None of it was. "I'm sorry." And I was, too. I'm not all bad. "You've got me all day. Let's see if we can come up with something else."

Paris looked at me, and after a moment he smiled. Good. Because this exterminator shit had to go. Especially the hard hats. Chicks don't dig hard-hat hair.

Two hours later we'd come up with a sadistic play on Nike's "Just Do It," and a terrible rendition of the Vegas ads: "What happens

with the Bombays stays with the Bombays."
Nothing clicked. We were just ripping off the
big boys.

Apparently my marketing skills were rusty.
After promising Paris that I would spend the
night thinking about our project, I called
Gin and arranged for her to pick up Louis
from school and keep him overnight (she
was thrilled, by the way). Then I headed to
my local public library to get some research
materials.

Apparently no one writes books on marketing for mom-and-pop assassination corpora-
tions. I found stuff on selling your retail,
nonprofit, Internet, wholesale, and general
services companies. There was guerrilla marketing, viral marketing, and other crap, but
nothing geared toward maintaining interest
from the same clients, and certainly nothing
on working with the CIA, Interpol, or others.

The closest I came was a book on the
management of death. No kidding. Its target
readership seemed to be funeral homes,
crematoriums, cemeteries, etc. Apparently
death was a growth industry. (Hmmm, death
and erectile dysfunction. I wonder if there
really is a conspiracy.) Still, I'd been here
three hours and come up with nothing, so I
reached for the book.

A tall redhead snatched it before I could.

She literally took the book out from under me, and it was the only copy.

"Hey!" I whined. "I was going to check that out!"

The woman turned to me. "So?" She frowned and began to walk away. *Oh, my God.* It was Leonie Doubtfire!

"Hey!" I shouted. My vocabulary had apparently abandoned me. "Wait a minute."

"Yes?" she asked a bit impatiently.

I was frozen. I didn't know what to do. She looked like a child or a woodland fairy. All of my atoms were riveted to the spot, and I couldn't move.

The redhead rolled her eyes and walked away. And I stood there like an idiot, saying nothing.

After about two minutes I uprooted myself and went back to the marketing section. I found myself in a daze, grabbing about five or six books at random and checking them out. Twenty minutes later I was sitting in my car trying to figure out what the hell had just happened.

She didn't remember me! *Me!* That had never happened before. Nope. Every woman I'd ever met remembered me. I stood out from the crowd. Women wanted me, dammit! Why didn't Leonie Doubtfire want me? And why hadn't I said *anything*? *Oh, my God!* I'd lost it. I'd really lost it!

When I got home I opened the yellow pages to *physicians*, *therapists*, *stylists*, and *priests*. My mojo, sexuality, and ego were AWOL. Obviously I needed some help.

Chapter Eight

"I bet it was that mouth that got you that nose."

— The Boss, *Lucky Number Slevin*

Gin called the next morning, informing me (not asking, mind you) that she and Liv were taking all the kids to the zoo for the day. They must have turned me in to the Bombay hotline, because Paris called within seconds, telling me I had one hour to get over there to work. I numbly agreed to all of the above and soon found myself back at my cousin's apartment.

"Mr. Skeevy died," Paris said as he opened the door.

"Who?" The name didn't sound like someone I'd killed recently. I'd remember a name like that. Hell, in my opinion you'd kill someone just because he had a name like that.

"You know—our old gym teacher," Paris

replied with a frown. He was doing a lot of that lately.

"Wow. I thought he was already dead." And I did too. Mr. Skeevy had been ancient when we were in school. I shuddered a little. He'd been a really weird dude. At more than six feet tall, Skeevy didn't take a lot of crap. He'd put in a long tour as a sniper in 'Nam and loved to bounce smart-ass boys off the lockers. Guess which kind of boy I was? I shuddered again, massaging my right shoulder.

He also had this unnerving habit of putting the starter pistol to his head, pulling the trigger, and shouting, "Try again, motherfuckers!" Where normal physical education consisted of dodgeball, track and field, and flag football, we played games like "Tet Offensive" and "Hanoi Hilton." Of course, that was before corporal punishment (and Chinese water torture) was banned from schools.

"The visitation's tonight. Funeral tomorrow," Paris continued.

"Don't tell me you're going!" I was kind of surprised. Skeevy was always harder on Paris. "Oh, I get it. You want to make sure he's dead."

"Yes, I'm going. But out of respect." Paris sniffed.

"Who are you? And where is the pod that holds Paris's body?"

He rolled his eyes. "Man, what is your problem? He wasn't that bad."

My eyebrows shot up. "Not that bad? He hated us!"

"No, he hated you. You teased him."

I sat back. "He always chose you to be the prisoner at the Hanoi Hilton!"

Paris's eyes flew open wide, and I wondered if I'd awakened a repressed memory. "God. Can you be serious for, like, five minutes? You really are an ass these days!"

Okay, he had me there. I was a snarky bastard. Paris was my best friend, but I'd had the bad habit of pushing him too far lately. I needed him.

"I'll go with you. Just don't expect any tears. After all, I wanted to kill him all through junior high."

We settled down to work, Paris on his laptop, me with the binders and pads of paper. That's how I like to brainstorm. We had only a few days left to come up with something brilliant, and I had to focus.

"What about giveaways?" Paris asked. I looked down at the paper and to my shock realized I'd been drawing a picture of the redhead from the bookstore.

"What do you mean?" I asked, casually trying to scribble out the picture.

"You know, some companies give out pens. Some give out calendars. Others do those stress squeezy thingies."

"You want us to give out calendars?" Now I knew the pod people had him. Wharton grads didn't hand out shit like that. Although we could do it as a gag to piss off the Council. Maybe we could do chimps in black suits with silenced pistols.

"Not necessarily. Maybe we could do those stress thingies in different shapes?"

I could just picture that. We could give out squeezy Colt .45s, or giant cyanide pills. *Riiiiiight.*

I pushed back from the table. "Apparently we're not only out of ideas—we never had any to begin with."

Paris sighed, and I knew I'd hit a nerve. "You're right. Slogans, logos, and promotional shit don't sell what we do."

"Results do. That's the only thing people in our line understand."

He nodded. "All right. So maybe instead of coming up with some slick campaign, we should find out why our results aren't making as big an impact on our clients."

"Yes. We could do some cost analysis and research into who our competition is." Now we were getting somewhere.

"But how do we find out about the other agencies? It's not like they'd run an ad in the yellow pages or have a Web site."

Hmmmm. He had a point. But for once I felt like we were on top of this. "I don't know. We'll just have to figure it out. We still have a few connections. Let's use them."

"Will that be enough for the Council?" Undoubtedly he was still holding on to the idea of squeezy thingies shaped like ice picks.

"If we can provide the solution, they'll be much happier. And we'll throw in a chimpanzee calendar for fun."

That night we changed clothes and headed to Skeevy's visitation. Mom had commandeered Louis from Gin, demanding grandma time, mumbling something about me not picking him up until Sunday night. To my surprise I felt a little sad about not seeing the kid for so long, but I shook it off. After all, Paris and I could hit the bars after the visitation and maybe I'd score. Hell, maybe I could pick up a hot little relative at the funeral home.

In spite of Skeevy I'd really dressed up. A navy Ralph Lauren blazer, gold shirt, red tie, and khakis, my hair tousled, and I looked like a prep-school smoothie. *Look out, ladies.*

Now, I don't spend a lot of time at funeral homes (you'd probably think I would, wouldn't you?), but I didn't even know this one existed. I mean, the name Crummy's Funeral Home would stand out. If any business needed a marketing plan, I'd think this one would. Although I thought it was perfect for Skeevy.

Why in the hell would anyone use a place called Crummy's? Even engraved Montblanc pens and little squeezy caskets wouldn't help sell this place. I laughed as we approached the door, realizing someone had bigger problems than Paris and I did.

The outside of the building was bland. It was just a one-story brick building with no embellishments. The inside was . . . well, beige. The carpet, walls, and furniture were beige. The art on the walls was different variations of beige. Even the morticians were dressed in taupe. *Yeesh. I know it's a death industry, but liven things up already.* The only person who didn't look like a zombie was a beige-suited young woman with flaming red hair.

"Good evening," said the redhead from the library somberly. Then she looked at me. "Oh, it's you."

I was completely stunned (and more than a little excited that she recognized me). Now I knew why she needed that book more than I did.

Paris introduced himself with great charm, to my strange irritation.

"Leonie Doubtfire." She shook Paris's hand, then reached for mine. "And you are?"

I said nothing, just stared at her hand as if it were a cobra ready to strike. (I say *cobra* affectionately. It was Great-great-uncle Arkansas's modus operandi—difficult to import, but very Cleopatra.)

Paris nudged me, and I clumsily grabbed her hand. "Bombay. Er . . . Dakota Bombay." *Jesus.* That was smooth. I'd never blown an introduction before.

"You must be with the Skeevy party," she said, and I nodded like an idiot. "They're in the Algonquin Room." She gave us a forced smile, then moved on to another couple who had just entered the funeral home.

All I could do was stand there, staring after her. My heart was beating a violent tattoo. What was wrong with me?

Paris nudged me again, and I shook myself out of the trance. He looked concerned but said nothing about my reaction. We followed the signs to the Algonquin Room and saw Old Skeevy laid out in his coffin at the head of the room. His family had chosen to bury him in his old gym uniform. Creepy. He still looked like hell. Seeing his corpse made me shudder, and I felt a ghost pain in my right shoulder. The geezer still scared the shit out of me after all of these years, in spite of the fact that he was dead and I was now a professional killer.

I turned my thoughts to more pleasant things, like Leonie Doubtfire. What a weird name. What a weird-looking chick. Why couldn't I get her out of my head?

"Hey," Paris whispered to me, "I've got two of Skeevy's nieces willing to hit the clubs with us later." I looked in the direction he pointed and saw two petite blondes (who obviously hadn't inherited anything from the deceased) wiggling their fingers at us.

"Yeah. Sure," I responded in a fog. I watched as he went over and told them I was in. They giggled with delight. It could be fun. As long as their idea of a drinking game wasn't Russian roulette, it might even be a good time.

For some reason I took the opportunity to flee the room. I wandered the hallways of Crummy's, looking for . . . for what? Maybe I just needed a break.

"So," Leonie said from behind me. "Come here often?"

I turned to face her, somewhat pissed off. "How do you know I'm not a relative of the deceased and would find your comment inappropriate?"

She shrugged and walked away. I was just about to go after her and apologize when Paris grabbed my arm and steered me toward the door, where the two Skeevy girls waited for us. As the four of us climbed into my car, I felt like a complete idiot. Maybe a little bamboo under the fingernails was what I deserved.

Chapter Nine

Prince Charmont: "You're the first maiden who hasn't swooned at the sight of me."
Ella of Frell: "Then maybe I've done you some good."

—*Ella Enchanted*

Saturday night was a total bust. It turned out the girls were Catholic (the real kind, not like the ones I knew in college who were Catholic only on Sundays) and didn't believe in fooling around. It was just as well: I wasn't interested. All I could think of was Leonie Doubtfire.

But why? She was totally against my type. The willowy redhead obviously wasn't blond, didn't fall all over me at first sight, and there was zero giggling. A little giggling always went a long way with me.

And that was why I was at the funeral home again the next morning for Skeevy's last hurrah.

"I don't get it," Paris whispered. "I thought

it was nice to go to the visitation, but why are we back?"

An old woman in a lilac polyester suit seated in the pew ahead turned around to glare at us.

"It's her, isn't it?" Paris persisted despite my attempts at ignoring him. He was pointing at Leonie.

"If you must know, yes. There's something about her I can't get out of my head."

"You came to a funeral just to pick up a mortician?" Paris asked.

Angry Lady in front turned around again. Apparently she disapproved. I ignored her.

"I just wanted to talk to her."

"Jesus, Dak," Paris replied.

Angry Lady turned around again. "Do you boys mind? This is a funeral!"

Paris apologized while I stuck my tongue out at her. Real mature, I know.

I caught up with the object of my confusion after the ceremony. Skeevy was being cremated—which seemed fitting—so there was no grave-site burial.

"Um, hey," I said gallantly. "Would you like to go out and get a cup of coffee or something?"

Leonie frowned. Why was everyone frowning at me lately? "Why?" she asked, reducing me to the size of a castrated ant.

"Why not?" was all my lame brain could come up with.

She stared at me for a moment, her light blue eyes sizing me up. I felt as if I were being inspected for maggot infestation.

"Sure," she said, and I let go of the breath I hadn't realized I was holding. "I'll meet you at the café on the corner in an hour." Then she turned and walked away.

I pretty much dragged Paris to the car, drove him to his house at eighty miles per hour, then returned to the café to wait for my coffee date. That left me with thirty minutes, most of which I spent finding the right casual pose in my chair.

Of course, the moment she walked in I realized I had a bigger problem: What was I going to say to her?

"It's Dakota, right?" she asked as she sat. Her smile was fleeting, causing me some doubt. But I reminded myself that she was here, after all. And that could only be seen as a plus.

I nodded. "And you are Leonie." *Ooh. Smooth.*

"Now that we have our names down, what should we talk about? I take it you didn't want to meet me to discuss your future funeral arrangements." Was that . . . Did I see a flash of a smile?

The words came to me as if Paris were my Cyrano, feeding me lines via radio from his car in the parking lot. Then I cursed myself for not thinking of having him do just that. "I wanted to apologize for yesterday. I was rude."

She waved her hand in the air. "Oh, that. No big. I figured you were just choked up."

Oh. Right. About Skeevy. Of course she'd think that. I was torn here because I didn't want *any* woman to think I was choked up over a creepy, geriatric gym teacher.

"Well, I also shouldn't have yelled at you at the library." And then my inner Daniel Webster dried up. Cyrano failed me. Leonie had better come up with something to say or this would be a long coffee date.

"Oh, yeah." She ran long white fingers through her blazing red curls. "I need that book. When I bought the mortuary I didn't realize I had to keep the name. So I'll take any help I can get."

"You bought Crummy's?"

"Just a few months ago. Moved here from Oregon. I thought I could make it work." She sighed and shook her head. Her lips had an adorable little pout that made me want to nibble on them. I held myself back.

"So you really are a mortician, then?"

Leonie narrowed her eyes at me. "Not really. It's just my cover. I'm trying to reanimate human life using parts of several dead people."

A joke. I liked that. "I guess that was a stupid question."

She nodded in agreement, and I felt my stock go down twenty points. "It's my family's business. That and I have a morbid fascination with death."

I could relate to that—carrying on the family business, working with dead people. (Actually, they weren't dead when I started working with them, but that's just plain nitpicking.)

"What brought you here?"

"I didn't want to work at the family's home. I thought I'd strike out on my own. I saw the ad for this place in our monthly industrial rag and just took a shot."

The conversation was so different from any other I'd had with a woman I was interested in. (Actually, there usually was very little conversation at all.) Leonie was serious, careerminded, and intelligent. None of these were qualities I typically looked for in a woman.

It took us two hours to get past the pleasantries. What surprised me was that I was having a good time.

Leonie looked at her watch. "Damn. I've got to run."

"So soon?" I asked, as if I didn't know we'd been there over two hours.

She nodded, and then something miraculous happened: She smiled. And I felt my insides turn into primeval ooze. Nothing any woman had ever done before made me feel so good. Weird, eh?

"Tell you what." She leaned forward and looked me in the eyes. "Why don't I take you out for dinner two nights from now?"

I used every atom in my body to keep from jumping on the table and dancing lewdly. "Great! How about Taschetta's at eight o'clock?"

Leonie smiled again. "I'll meet you there." And then she left.

I was so exhausted and spent I thought I'd just come from an all-night orgy. (Man, I missed those parties.) Who knew women could be interesting? And a date. How cool was that? Maybe things were looking up!

After a few little Gene Kelly hops on the light posts outside (no rain though, which was good because it would have mussed my perfect hair), I finally made it to my car. I picked up Louis and a pizza, and the two of us watched *X-Men* movies until I realized it was way past his bedtime. Mom had told me to make it eight p.m., but it was well past ten already. I tucked my son into his bed, then collapsed into mine. My last thoughts before sleep claimed me were of Leonie and her pretty little pout.

* * *

"What's this?" I asked Louis in regard to the yellow flier he handed me after school. Gin, Liv, and I sat on benches at the school's playground.

"It's a notice from the principal." Louis eyed me sternly. Romi and Alta shouted for him, and he ran off to play.

I scanned the note with a bit of awe. I was a parent now. I got important, goldenrod-colored memos from the school. How cool was that?

But something in the words made me read it again.

"What the hell?" I said aloud. Gin shushed me and I waved her off. "It says they're banning the games of tag and flag football for being too violent." I looked at my sister and cousin. "Did you see this?"

Gin and Liv had the contents of their children's backpacks sprawled on the benches beside them. I made an effort to emulate them without really knowing why—other than that must be what all the cool parents did.

"Unbelievable," Gin cried. "It says running has the potential to cause collisions. And pulling the flags off the belt can result in chafing."

Liv nodded grimly. "I've heard of this. It's already going on in other states. I'm afraid this is what we're heading toward."

I rolled my eyes. "Why? Does this make any sense?"

Gin replied, "Not to us. But the local schools have been getting more safety conscious lately."

I made a face. "In thirty years have you ever heard of anyone maimed on this playground?" Again they shook their heads. "I don't remember anyone dying from playing tag. It would be all over the news."

Gin cocked her head to the side. "It would be. Kid dies in bizarre tag collision. Children severed at the waist from tight flag-football belts."

"Pretty soon the kids won't even get to play on the playground," Liv chimed in. "All they'll be allowed to do at recess is stand up against the building."

"That's fucked up"—I ignored Gin's shushing—"'cause this stuff is safer than what we had. Now they have soft rubber mats. We had skin-shredding gravel underneath."

Gin nodded. "And all the equipment is molded plastic with no seams or edges. We had splintered wood and rusty, jagged metal."

"Don't forget the kind of equipment," Liv added. "Merry-go-rounds that spun you into another county, two-story-tall slides with rickety ladders, butt-busting teeter-totters. None of those things even exist now."

She had a point. "Hell, we didn't even have helmets to ride our bikes with, elbow and knee pads for roller skating, car seats, or use seat belts."

Gin added, "And yet I don't remember a single kid dying on any of those things when we were growing up."

I snorted. "Too bad we didn't have to take out any other kids back then. Apparently playgrounds would've made very useful death traps, and we didn't even know it."

Liv and Gin shot me looks that burned through my skull, blowing a big, figurative hole out the back of my head.

"So what do we do about this?" I asked.

Gin shook her head. "I don't know. What do you think, Liv?"

Liv squinted up at the sky. "Well, we are card-carrying members of the PTA. I guess we could attend the next meeting and protest?"

That sounded too difficult, too boring, and too administrative. "Let's kill the PTA president . . . make an example of him and demand they rescind this." Now, that was well within my skill set.

For a moment I thought my sister and cousin were actually going to consider it.

"I'd give anything to do that, little brother." Gin sighed.

"Why? Who's the president?"

"Vivian Marcy," Liv said.

Oh, shit. No wonder Gin wanted to kill her. That bitch had been horrible to my sister when they were growing up.

I didn't like her either. Once she discovered I was Gin's little brother, she tormented me too. Her nickname for me was "Dorkota." Thank God I became a stud in high school or I'd have never lived that down.

"How the hell did she get to be in charge of the PTA?" I asked.

Gin turned to me without missing a beat. "She seduced Satan and had his baby, enrolling the incubus at Kennedy."

"Or she killed the previous PTA president and took his place," Liv countered.

This lively discussion went on for some time. I sat back and watched Louis playing with the girls. He was showing them how to construct a DNA double helix using leftovers from their lunches. Who knew there were so many uses for Twizzlers and Cheetos balls?

Damn, that kid was smart. As I sat there I felt a sharp surge of affection for him. I was getting those a lot lately. Maybe this dad gig wasn't bad. Maybe someday he'd dedicate his Nobel Peace Prize to me.

Of course, he wouldn't be a scientist. Louis was a Bombay now. And at six years old he was a year late in beginning his training as an assassin. Any day now Grandma could summon us to Santa Muerta for the blood-letting ceremony.

It wasn't fair. I just got him, and I'd have to start turning him into a killer. Of course, then we'd have a lot more to worry about than flag-football chafing. *Damn.*

Chapter Ten

"I came up with a new game-show idea recently. It's called *The Old Game*. You got three old guys with loaded guns onstage. They look back at their lives, see who they were, what they accomplished, how close they came to realizing their dreams. The winner is the one who doesn't blow his brains out. He gets a refrigerator."

—Chuck Barris, *Confessions of a Dangerous Mind*

"Why am I doing this again?" Louis looked up from the pieces of the .45 that littered my dining room table. I'd decided to start some of his training that night, so I'd disassembled the gun to show him how to take it apart and clean it. Well, that and I still hadn't cleaned it from the last job. Mom had never tolerated dirty guns in the house when we were kids. Our rooms could look like they were trashed by the Sex Pistols, but guns had to be spotless twenty-four/seven.

"I'm just teaching you about guns." Okay, I'm a chickenshit coward. I thought I'd start small and wait until the blood ceremony to fill him in on everything.

Louis poked the bore brush through the gun barrel, sliding it in and out to loosen the dirt. He glanced up at me suspiciously but didn't say a word.

Mom showed up for her nightly I-have-to-make-sure-you-are-raising-my-grandson-right ritual. She frowned when she saw said grandson putting my .45 back together. I was pretty impressed he'd picked it up so quickly. She dragged me by the elbow into the other room.

"What are you doing?" Mom hissed.

"What?" I rubbed my elbow. "I'm starting his training."

"He's not ready! The poor kid just joined the family!"

"I know. I'm starting slow. I haven't given him the lowdown yet, just asked him to help me clean the gun. That's all." *God!* What was her problem?

Mom stuck around for dinner. Apparently Dad was fending for himself while she whipped up a three-course meal for me and Louis. I was actually surprised I had vegetables in my kitchen. Louis hugged her when she was finished, and I did the dishes while she put him to bed with a story.

Finally I got Mom out the door and tucked him in myself.

"Louis," I started, brushing some of his hair from his forehead. I screwed up my courage to ask him, "What was life with your mom like?"

"It was all right. She was a stewardess, so we moved around a lot. Mom told me her family was dead. I found out later that they weren't. They were just Republicans."

"Do you like it here?"

He nodded. "Yup. I love having a big family. The school is pretty good—even if it doesn't have a talented-and-gifted program. And Grandma's a good cook." He grinned crookedly, the gap between his two front teeth pronounced. How goddamned cute was that?

"Well, I hope I can be a good dad. I'm not used to this, you know? But I'll figure it out."

Louis rolled his eyes. "Duh. But it's okay. It's a steep learning curve. Besides, it's not like life with Mom was normal. Nitroglycerin is more stable than that."

I laughed. My kid made a joke—albeit a science geek/genius joke, but a joke nonetheless. "Good night, Louis." I kissed him on the forehead.

"Night, Dad." He winked, then rolled over and closed his eyes.

I couldn't sleep that night. There were too many things on my mind. Life used to be so simple. Kill one or two guys a year, sleep with more than a hundred blondes a year, no pets, no commitments, and lots of play money.

After tossing and turning in bed I got up and wandered through my condo with the lights off. I liked it like that. It was so quiet. Like it used to be all the time, actually.

Shadows dozed throughout the living room, and I sank down on the couch to watch the lights change as cars went by. It was weird to be wearing silk boxer shorts. I'd been a total nudist all of my life (to Gin's teenage horror and her sleepover friends' delight). But with a young, impressionable boy in the house, I thought I'd cover up somewhat.

Maybe I just needed to think. In all honesty I hadn't had much time to do that. Not that I was ever much of a thinker. When your philosophy in life is, "What the hell?" you don't tend to ponder the big questions like, "Why are we here?" (Although for many years I labored under the impression that I was here to be utterly adorable and give pleasure to women.)

Things change. Now I had a different purpose. Maybe it was time to finally settle down. You know, be a dad to Louis and a lover to Leonie—maybe more. These thoughts kept spinning around in my head as I sat there in the dark.

I had a split second to react to the glint of light I saw out of the corner of my eye. I wasn't alone. Fortunately the idiot didn't know I was there.

I slowly turned my head in his direction, careful not to make the springs in the couch creak. There was a guy in my living room! And I'd say from the dark clothing and stocking cap he didn't enter my house by accident.

In my bare feet it was easy to get the jump on him before he saw me. Creeping up behind the bastard, I carefully lifted a sculpture off my coffee table and brained him with it. He hit the floor with a thud—no idea what had happened. I looked at the statue of the nude woman in my hand. There was a little crater where her head used to be. *Damn.* I really liked that piece. Then it occurred to me that I probably shouldn't have stuff like this with Louis around. I toyed with hitting the thug again, but decided against it.

"Unhhhhhh . . ." The prowler started to come to, just in time to notice my incredible handiwork integrating rope with the kitchen chair. Scoutmaster Thompson would be so proud of me.

I'd already pulled his wallet. What a dumb-ass. You don't take your wallet on a job!

"Hey, Bobby John!" I said brightly as he squinted at me. "Yes, your head hurts, and no, I won't untie you so you can touch it. You'll just have to trust me on this one."

Bobby John Drake's eyes grew really wide. If this were just a simple breaking and entering, he didn't expect this. I let him panic a little—which he did rather impressively, once he discovered he was completely naked—before continuing. This was an old trick Uncle Pete taught me: When you're naked, you feel completely vulnerable.

"So, Bobby John." I clapped him on the shoulder amiably. "What brings you to my house at"—I looked at the clock—"two a.m.?" I smiled charmingly.

"What the hell, man?" Bobby John whined.

"I beg your pardon?" I asked.

"Why the hell have you tied me up? And what did you do to me?" Tough words. Unfortunately they were punctuated with nervous squeaks.

I sat in a chair across from him. While he was out I'd taken the opportunity to dress in jeans, a black cashmere pullover, and loafers. I hoped he appreciated the irony of our role reversal.

"You ever seen *Reservoir Dogs*, Bobby John?" I asked.

He gulped, like they do in cartoons. "Yeah."

"Remember that scene with Michael Madsen and the cop he has tied to a chair?" I laughed. It was a good scene. A bit graphic when he cuts the cop's ear off with the straight razor, but still good.

Bobby John responded by wetting himself. Good thing I had solid wood chairs and linoleum flooring. Apparently he had seen that movie.

"So, anyway"—I drew my right leg up, ankle on my left knee—"what are you doing in my house?" I asked casually enough. It wasn't my fault the man started crying.

"Shit! Shit!" he sputtered. But no answers.

I got up and walked over to my silverware drawer, pulling it open. "I don't have a straight razor, Bob. You don't mind if I call you Bob, do you? It's just that calling a grown man Bobby John makes me want to torture someone." I pulled a butter knife from the drawer.

"I do have a dull knife, though. I s'pose I could do more damage with that anyway."

"It's just a job, man!" Bob wept.

I sat across from him again. "What job would that be?"

No response.

I slapped my head. "You know what?" I got up and snagged a fork and a hot dog, bringing them back to the table next to him. "I think I could cause a lot more pain with a fork." I stuck the fork into the uncooked meat and raked it lengthwise until I had completely shredded the wiener.

"Some guy paid me to do it!" the man squealed. "I don't know who! He just gave me five hundred dollars to come in and check out your place!" The tears were flowing now, and Bob's skin was turning an alarming shade of red.

I crossed my arms. "Right. What a terrible cliché, Robert. You don't mind if I call you Robert, do you? It's just that I get the giggles when I say the name Bob. Did you know that's a palindrome? It's spelled the same way forward and backward."

"I swear! That's it! I don't even know his name!"

"How were you going to report what you found back to him then?"

Bob's head looked as if it were going to explode. He started to scream, and I gave him a right hook to the jaw.

"Sorry about that, Robert. I can't have you waking the neighbors." I didn't want to tell him I had my son a short distance away.

Bob nodded like he understood, then continued: "He was going to e-mail me. That's how I got the job in the first place."

I stared at him. "You took a job from a stranger over the Internet?" What a loser. If you can't meet them face-to-face, it's probably a setup. Grandma always said that if it seems too good to be true, it probably is. Good old Grandma. I really love the gal. Well, except for when she's been trying to kill me.

Bob sniffled. "I needed the money." And I had to agree. His now-missing wardrobe looked like he shopped in the stealth section of Dollar General. "I wasn't gonna hurt you. Just find out who all lived here and the layout. That's it."

I sighed and pulled the blue Springfield Armory .45 from the back of my jeans and placed it on the table. Bob's eyes almost burst.

"That's all you know?" I asked patiently.

There was a moment of silence, and I toyed with bringing up the pawnshop scene from *Pulp Fiction*, but Bob seemed to be telling the truth. He was just a broke, two-bit loser who did something stupendously stupid—like break into the condo of a professional assassin. Of course, he didn't know that.

"What's this guy's e-mail address? Does he have a name?" I asked, talking to Bob but looking at the pistol. I loved that gun. It was a gift from Mom on my fifteenth birthday. It was unregistered, of course, and came with a hand-tooled calfskin holster.

He didn't miss a beat. "Says his name's Doc Savage."

If I were a dog, Bob would've seen my ears

prick up. "Really? The Man of Bronze?" My inner ten-year-old geek kicked in, and I was suddenly transported to my parents' attic, knee-deep in Kenneth Robeson novels.

Bob squinted at me. "That name mean something to you?"

"I believe I'm the one in charge of this inquisition, Mr. Drake. You don't mind if I call you Mr. Drake, do you? I do prefer to distance myself from my victims."

I smiled as he shuddered. The name did, in fact, mean something to me. I'd always wanted to be just like Doc Savage: independently wealthy, surrounded by willing and knowledgeable henchmen, blond hair and glowing tan, scouring the world for evil. I'd read all the books and seen the Ron Ely movie a million times. I even wanted a 1930s roadster for my first car, but Mom said it would stand out too much. Bombays never call attention to themselves. So instead of a cool car, I got what all the other kids got—a stupid Chevy Citation.

"That's all I know," Bob stammered, "I . . . I . . . I swear!"

I knew he was telling me the truth. There was nothing more to get out of Bob. I slapped a piece of duct tape over his mouth and held a liberal dose of Gin's special knockout drug over his nose until he passed out.

He'd be unconscious for at least ten hours, easy. But what should I do with him? I mean, I couldn't let my little boy come to breakfast to find an unconscious naked man tied to a chair. After about ten minutes of intense thinking, I dragged him into the cleaning closet, threw a blanket over him, and locked the door. That should hold Bobby John Drake till I figured out what the hell to do with him. The question was, what did this all mean?

"Um, Dad?" Louis stood in the doorway of the kitchen, his small fists rubbing sleepy eyes.

I felt a little twinge inside my heart. I was starting to love it when he called me Dad. "What is it? You should be in bed."

Louis looked around the kitchen, then frowned. "One of the chairs is missing, and it smells like a dog peed in here." His eyes rested on mine. "We don't have a dog."

I know you are supposed to be honest with kids, but I couldn't think of a logical explanation. So I went with the next best thing— making him think he was hallucinating. Putting my hands on his shoulders, I turned him gently toward his room.

"All four chairs are there, and no one had an accident on the floor. You're still dreaming. Back to bed now."

To my immense relief Louis shrugged and went back to his room, shutting the door behind him. After cleaning up the kitchen, I sat in the living room for a long time trying to figure out what to do next.

A couple of hours later, as I fed my son his Lucky Charms (they *are* magically delicious) in the living room so he wouldn't notice the missing chair in the kitchen, I still didn't have a clue. Zip, zero, *nada*. Not one single idea what to do with the man in my cleaning closet. When I got back home from dropping Louis off at school, I pulled Drake out of the closet, still attached to the chair.

He stared at me while I dragged him to the kitchen and whimpered as I pulled the tape off of his mouth.

"Okay," I said amiably, "where were we?"

Bobby John Drake shook his head, indicating he wasn't much of a talker as of late.

"What kind of grown man goes around as Bobby John?" I asked him. When he didn't respond, I continued: "Not interested in talking?"

"I don't have nothing else to say."

"That's too bad." I started looking through cupboards. "Now, where did I put that rusty ice pick?"

"I told you all I know!" Bob squealed.

You know what? I believed him. How about that?

"So what do you suggest I do with you?" I asked calmly. Normally I don't give my victims a chance. They always have to die. But I was feeling a little magnanimous.

"Let me go! I won't tell Savage anything! I didn't get very far anyway!"

"Do you know the significance of the name Doc Savage?"

Bob shook his head.

I sighed. "Too bad for you," I answered as I hit him with the frying pan I never used. As he slumped forward, I thought I probably shouldn't use it to make my son pancakes anytime soon.

For your information, Bobby John woke up several hours later, naked and penniless, on top of a Dumpster outside a biker bar in east St. Louis. Hey, at least he wasn't dead.

Chapter Eleven

(Practicing in a mirror before his high school reunion.)

"Hi, I'm Martin Blank; you remember me? I'm not married, I don't have any kids, and I'd blow your head off if someone paid me enough."

—Martin Blank, *Grosse Pointe Blank*

"You're such a normal guy," Leonie said before shoving a forkful of fettuccine into her mouth.

"No, not really." And she would know that if she'd been at my house at two a.m. to see Bobby John naked and tied to a chair in my kitchen. But she wasn't. We were at my favorite Italian restaurant having a typical, average date. It was only natural that she'd think I was normal. Of course, I wasn't sure what a mortician's idea of normal was.

Leonie nodded. "Sure you are."

No, I'm not. "You just haven't gotten to know me yet," I replied.

Leonie rested her head in her hand. "Let me guess: good college, white-collar degree with postgraduate work, thinks he's God's gift to women, and prefers blondes."

"Shows what you know. I'm an agnostic." Maybe my cologne gave me away? Or was it the Italian loafers? I was pretty sure it wasn't my hair. I'd achieved perfection in that arena.

"So, am I right?" She smiled, and I thought about taking her right there on the table. Of course, I would not be welcome here again.

"Somewhat. I have a master's in marketing from an Ivy League school. I'm a consultant. And I'll admit to a less-than-healthy respect for blondes. But that was before I met you."

Leonie smiled again, and my blood pressure skyrocketed. Suddenly I forgot what color blonde was.

"Well, maybe I can hire you to help me with Crummy's."

I felt a sharp stab of guilt. I'd left Paris pretty much in the lurch, and we had to go to Santa Muerta for our presentation in just a few days. He was even babysitting for me tonight. I made a mental note to make it up to him tomorrow. Flowers? Wine? Maybe one of the blondes at Gin's spa?

"Okay, but my prices can be steep."

Leonie laughed. Dinner went beautifully. By the time dessert rolled around we were swapping bad pickup lines.

"I think my favorite has to be, 'Nice shoes. Wanna fuck?'" Leonie said with a smirk.

"You're kidding. Someone actually used that on you?" *Hmmm.* I'd have to write that one down later.

She nodded. "And I was wearing hiking boots at the time." She took a drink from her glass of wine. "I'm having a great time, Dakota."

I smiled. "Me too. And you can call me Dak."

"So, what's up next, Dak?" she asked with a wicked grin. I knew what I wanted to do. But did morticians do that on the first date?

A strange beeping noise broke into my fantasy involving Leonie and me naked . . . anywhere. This would be my first time with a redhead. It almost made me feel like a virgin all over again.

"Shit," Leonie said.

Oh. The beeping came from her. I watched as she pulled a cell phone from her purse. Leonie frowned at it before putting it away.

"I'm sorry, Dak. I've got to go. People are so inconsiderate—dying at the most inopportune moments."

Oh. Right. In her line of work she probably got calls at all kinds of weird hours.

I tried to hide my disappointment. "It's okay. You go, and I'll take care of the check." I rose from my seat.

Leonie came around to my side of the table, threw her arms around me, and kissed me hard on the lips. She smelled like rose water and vanilla and tasted like cabernet. I reached up and tangled my hands in her hair, kissing her as if I were devouring chocolate. I wanted her so badly I thought maybe the stiff (as opposed to my stiffy) could wait. What's a few hours when you're already dead, anyway?

Finally she pulled away. "You're a peach, Dak! I'll make it up to you!" And then she was gone.

My head was spinning as I paid the tab, grotesquely overtipped the waiter, and flew through the air to Paris's place.

"Hello, Paris, my man!" I swung the door open wide and danced into the living room. Louis was curled up asleep on the sofa.

"Isn't he the greatest kid ever?" I beamed at my son.

Paris raised one eyebrow. "Are you drunk?"

"No, I'm not!" I took my best friend and cousin in my arms and started waltzing him around the room.

He pulled away. "Oh, my God. It's happened. I owe Liv two thousand dollars."

I stopped and looked at him. "What's that?"

"Nothing," he rushed. "We only have two

days till we leave for Santa Muerta. I'll expect you right after you take Louis to school in the morning."

"Fine," I answered as I scooped the boy up into my arms and carried him to the car. Once in bed, I thought for a brief moment about what Paris had said, then traded in those thoughts for fantasies about Leonie, her kisses, and her long red hair.

"Did you say something about owing Liv money last night?" I asked Paris when I got to his place the next day.

Paris chuckled—presumably at my expense. "Yeah. Liv and I made a bet ten years ago that you'd never fall in love. As you got older, the pot grew higher."

I stared at him. "You bet money on that?"

He nodded. "And it looks like I lost, by the way you were acting last night."

"I am not in love with Leonie. It's a phase. I find her career choice . . . interesting."

"Riiiiiiiiiight." Paris had a smug look on his face, and I really wanted to punch it off.

"Let's just get to work," I snapped. Now, why in the hell would it bother me to think I had feelings for Leonie? I shoved that thought aside for now. We had work to do.

Paris typed into his laptop. "Okay. You had

the right idea wondering why our assignments have decreased. I called a few contacts, and it seems that there's another firm competing with the Bombays." He slid the notebook over to me.

"National Resources?" I frowned at the generic name on the generic Web site in front of me. "What does that mean?"

"Nothing, presumably. There's no mention of who they are or what they do. Just a hidden e-mail address I can't hack into."

"Who did you talk to at the agencies?" I asked, not taking my eyes off the bland screen with nothing but a contact button.

"Neil over at Langley. Anders at Mossad."

"Ha!" I snorted. "Remember that time the four of us got so drunk we woke up in Bogotá wearing lederhosen?" *Good times.*

"Yeah. I remember that. Especially the part where you tried to sell me to that pair of white slavers from Yemen."

Oh. He remembered that. "Moving on . . ." I mumbled. To be honest, I wasn't really going to sell Paris to those guys. It was just a fraternity prank. Although Ali and his brother weren't terribly amused at the time.

"Anyway, National Resources underbid us a few years back on a case. The agencies have been using them ever since."

"When were Neil and Anders gonna tell us?" I was pissed. The four of us had been really close since we had shared the same dorm room freshman year. Now that I thought of it, it was kind of weird how we all ended up in the professions we did.

Paris shook his head. "It wasn't easy to get that out of them. I had to use blackmail. I still have those photos of them posing with Air Supply at the concert in Milan."

I laughed. We really came down on them when we found out they ditched us at the brothel to meet Air Supply. I mean, come on! Air Supply?

"Neil says these guys are good. They're also cheaper than we are, and they wear suits when they make their hits. That's why our contracts are down."

"Grandma's gonna be pissed. Especially since they have a Web site."

Paris looked pretty grave. "She called. The meeting's been moved up. We're expected in Santa Muerta tomorrow. And there's something else."

"Tomorrow? I can't do tomorrow! I have a date with Leonie! And what about Louis? I can't ditch him for a couple of days!" I, Dakota Bombay, started to panic. I'd never really had any reason to turn Grandma down before. Well, there was that time I was on a ski trip in Aspen, but I made it back before the three Austrian nurses got cold.

"You have to bring Louis. She wants to meet him."

Oh, shit. "She knows about Louis?" I wasn't ready for that.

Paris nodded. "She wants Missi to run a DNA test on him while we're there."

I slumped into my chair. A DNA test. Of course she'd want that. In the Council's paranoid brain, Louis could be a midget spy. They'd have to make sure he was of the Bombay blood. Missi was the family's version of James Bond's Q. There would be no margin for error in her results.

"I really like Louis," Paris said. "I'm sure the test will prove he's your son."

He was telling the truth. I knew that. Paris may have been irritated with me lately, but he was still my right-hand dude. And of course he and Louis had hit it off. They were a lot alike. But it was what he said that struck me. I never really believed that Louis wasn't mine. And if he wasn't a true Bombay, what would the Council do with him? He would have been to Santa Muerta, and with that kid's brains, they wouldn't allow him to leave. Not alive, anyway.

I wasn't going into this with just Paris hav-

ing my back. The Council was ruthless—
even though they were family (or maybe especially *because* they were family). They'd
threatened to kill my niece, Romi, just six
months ago. They wouldn't hesitate to take
Louis out of the picture. He'd be seen only as
a threat to them.

I dug my cell phone out of my pocket and
dialed. There was only one person who could
help me now: Mom.

Chapter Twelve

Hannibal King: "We call ourselves the Nightstalkers."
Blade: "Sounds like a reject from a Saturday-morning cartoon."
Hannibal King: "Well, we were going to go with the Care Bears, but that was taken."

—Trinity

The next day found me, my son, my mother, and my cousin on the family's private jet headed to Bombay HQ—the island of Santa Muerta. I'm not sure how long the family has had the island. It's my understanding that no one was really interested in meeting in our own homes. I mean, who wants an army of assassins (isn't it bad enough that they're family?) over for a potluck? Consider yourself lucky all *you* have to endure is dry turkey, instant potatoes, and Aunt Katy's incontinence problem. At Christmas, when I was sixteen, Uncle Lou used me to demonstrate a new choke hold he developed that rendered you unconscious in half the time.

"You're a big, strapping kid now!" I recall Lou saying as he dragged me over to him. I had bruises for a month. (I told everyone they were hickeys, of course.)

Where was I? Oh, yeah. So the Bombay family just started coming up with excuses for not hosting reunions, holidays, etc. You know, stuff like, "Our metal detector's down," and the old standby, "With a house full of weapons and two teenagers going through puberty, this isn't a good time for us." And using the neighboring church or community center was out. Somewhere along the line one of my relatives found an island named Saint Death and said, "That's it!"

No one ever lived on the island before us. Well, I guess that's not entirely true. A bunch of sailors were shipwrecked there a long time ago and decided that murdering and eating one another was a good alternative to coconuts. The mainlanders didn't seem to think the island juju was good, so we swooped in and got it for a song. Yay, us.

When I was growing up I thought it was pretty cool that our family owned an island. Paris and I loved running through the jungle, catching crabs on the beach, and shooting high-powered sniper rifles at a dummy in a car from a rooftop in a mock city—you know, the typical boys-of-summer thing. I only recently discovered that Paris had a secret tunnel he used to sneak off to when he was poetically inclined. But that's another story.

We liked to pretend this was Dr. Benton Quest's secret island, although we always fought over who was Jonny and who had to be Hadji. Too bad we didn't have a Race Bannon. During our training I guess Mom filled that bill. But she refused to wear a white crew cut (no matter how much we begged), and it was disturbing to imagine Race in a jumper decorated with kittens (insert shudder here).

The island has it all. A large, resort building with rooms for every member of the family (keyed in to our biometrics, of course, so we don't have to mess with keys or plastic cards—I hate those). All the resort amenities are there—pool, staff that understands only Spanish (all men, though—I always wondered why), and a penthouse for each member of the Council.

The Council lived on Santa Muerta on and off. My cousin Missi and her twin sons, Monty and Jack; her mother, Cali; and grandmother, Dela, lived there year-round. They took care of the general upkeep, etc. The rest of us Bombay rabble visited only when summoned or for the family reunions every five years.

You think your family reunion is lame? Try

a Bombay reunion. The resort is equipped with a customized conference center with auditorium. We have meals and meetings, but instead of the sack race, we have a full ropes course for team building. The only Bombays I trust are my immediate family. But on the ropes course you have to pick relatives you don't see much. I've never seen so many twitchy trigger fingers in my life. (As you can imagine, weapons aren't allowed.)

The island also has a private airstrip and dock, and south of the resort are a handful of luxury beachside cabins we can use. It was a great place—until my teenage libido kicked in, since there are no girls. I stopped going there just for fun. Too bad too. It would have been a great makeout hideaway.

"You're going to meet Great-grandma Maryland!" Mom said brightly with Louis safely tucked away on her lap, a blissed-out smile on his little mug.

The way she said that sounded like we were just going over the river and through the woods to a little clapboard house with a picket fence, musty doilies, and home-baked cookies. Not the chic penthouse of an old woman who could snap a man's neck like dry pasta. Mom had really blown a fuse when I told her that Grandma wanted to inspect Louis. It would be good to have her

with us. Mom was still chafing from not be-
ing there when Gin had to rescue Romi from
Grandma and the Council six months ago.
And honestly, in a death match between
Mom and Grandma, my money's on Mom.
Every time.

"Great Grandma lives on an island in the
southern hemisphere?" Louis asked for, like,
the fiftieth time. This wasn't a kid you could
baby-talk and lie to.

"Yup," I answered. "You'll like it on Santa
Muerta." *As long as my family doesn't try to
kill you.*

"And we have our own jet?" Louis raised
his right eyebrow.

I nodded.

"Why does everyone have place names?"

"Well, it's a family tradition dating back for
centuries," Mom answered patiently. She's so
good with kids. Mom then told him about
Uncle Louisiana, Uncle Petersburg, Aunt Virginia, my cousin Mississippi, and her sons,
Montgomery and Jackson. Most of us shortened our first name as soon as possible. My
sister, Gin, was Ginny until college, when
everyone (me included) thought it was funnier for her to be Gin Bombay.

I still hadn't given my son the whole run-
down on the family. At this point I figured

that monosyllabic responses and head nods were the safest route.

We landed on the airstrip on the island after flying all day. I was nervous. And this was unusual for me. In my whole life I'd never taken being a Bombay very seriously. Of course, unlike Gin or Liv (short for Liverpool), I never had to introduce outsiders to the lifestyle of the rich and deadly.

But now I was worried, and most of it was for my son. I felt a twinge of affection. Louis was my son. How cool is that? Hey, he has a place name too! But don't think I'm adding "Saint" to it. That would be ridiculous.

"Dak!" Missi came running toward the plane and threw her arms around me, then Paris, then Mom. "And is this Louis?" She bent down and hugged my kid, and he responded with a big, gap-toothed grin.

"I'm your dad's cousin. You can call me Missi." She took Louis by the hand. "The Council's in the auditorium, waiting for you two." She pointed at me and Paris. "Carolina, you can come with us, if you like." She smiled broadly at Mom. Yeah, like Mom was going to let Louis out of her sight.

I loved Missi. She was kind of odd, but then, who isn't in this family? Petite with short blond hair, Missi is maybe six or seven years older than I am. She'd lost her husband when the twins were two years old, but managed to raise her teenage boys and still keep her sense of humor. I had a lot of respect for her. Especially when she electrocuted the Council just as they were about to gun us down. That woman has foresight.

Mom nodded and took Louis's other hand, and it was good to know he'd be safe. Of course, I trusted Missi implicitly. She was a good egg. It was the rest of the family I wasn't so sure about.

"Well," Paris said with a sigh, "here goes nothing."

I nodded, and silently we went into the main building and down to the conference center.

It was satisfying to see the members of the Council visibly flinch when Paris and I entered the room. Obviously they remembered our last visit. Lou, Grandma, Dela(ware), Troy, and Flo(rence) sat on the dais. I wondered if Missi had ever told them they were secretly implanted with electric devices that could zap them into twitching seniors. My guess was that she hadn't.

The Council had existed in the Bombay family since the beginning of our venture into the profitable world of assassination. Consisting of the five eldest members, they hand out assignments and keep the business running smoothly. My grandmother Maryland; her brother, Lou; and their sister, Dela, form the American branch of the family. Their cousins, Troy and Florence, are the Europeans, from England and France, respectively. I guess I never really thought about the Council much—that is, until they had Gin hunt down the family mole. The Council is also responsible for "punishing" errant Bombays. And by "punishing" I don't mean a spanking. These bastards are old and bitter and totally committed to the Bombay way of life. They would eat their own young to keep everything in working order.

"What do you have to report?" Grandma broke into my thoughts.

"Nice to see all of you, too," I replied glibly. *Yeesh.* Where were their manners?

"We found out why our contracts are decreasing," Paris piped up. *Brownnose.*

"I'm fine, thanks for asking," I continued. "Have a new girlfriend and a son now."

"We know all about that," sneered Troy, the English member of the Council. "The question is, what do you have to report?"

Those Brits—no sense of humor.

Paris filled them in on National Resources. He told them everything. I would have left out the part about the Web site, but that's just me.

Lou frowned. "So, they have a Web site, eh? I knew we should've gotten one of those."

Grandma looked at me. "Did you come up with the branding I asked for?"

"Oh, sure. We thought about calling ourselves Assassinations R Us and aligning ourselves with the toy magnate. We figure we could just glom onto their brand and surf the success."

Grandma narrowed her eyes. "That'll do, Dak. I won't tolerate your snarky attitude." *Uh-oh.* I was getting dangerously close to not being spoiled by her.

Paris broke in. "We figured that by finding the real problem, we could come up with a better solution. The problem isn't really branding or Web sites or promotional tchotchkes. It's the competing company itself."

"So you're saying that if we take out the competition, our problem will cease?" Dela asked.

Oooooh. It's a trap! Don't answer that, Paris!

Paris looked confused but nodded. "Well, yes. That would solve the problem."

Troy shook his head, and I hated him all over again. "We know all about National Resources. You wasted your time."

"You knew about them?" I lost my cool. "Why didn't you tell us?"

Lou cleared his throat. Clearly we made a bit of an impact on the Council last time we were there. "Calm down, Dak."

"Calm down? Calm down? Are you crazy? We did all that work for nothing?" Okay, so Paris did all that work for nothing.

The members of the Council, my family, looked at one another. I was totally pissed off. Why give us the problem to solve when they knew the answer?

"Why don't we just have Dak and Paris remove the competition from the picture?" Dela suggested. "It seems silly to market ourselves when we're supposed to be a covert operation anyway."

"I agree. This nonsense about branding won't solve anything," piped up Aunt Florence, my French relative.

"Actions do speak louder than words, old man," Troy agreed grudgingly as he turned to Lou.

Grandma leveled an angry glare at him. "I want a complete marketing package! I want a Web site and logos and slogans!" *Damn*. Was she throwing a temper tantrum?

"Okay, Veruca Salt," Lou sniped. I tried to hide my smile. "But basically I agree that we need to get rid of them. What's to stop them from trying to take us out in the near future?

They underbid us—so why wouldn't they come after us?"

I stepped forward. "Give us all the info you have on this generic cabal, and Paris and I will take care of it. Do you want us to recruit others, like Gin or Liv?" Maybe I could earn some brownie points with my gift-bestowing grandmother in the process.

"No," Dela answered. "Let's keep this simple. You two can take out five men, can't you? If we put too many family members on this it'll be a mess."

Grandma folded her arms over her chest. "Fine. The two of you will meet with Dela tonight in her room. She'll give you what we have and you can take it from there."

I left the room totally pissed off. If the Council knew about the competition, why ask us to go around the problem with a slick promo plan?

"We should have killed them all last time we were here," Paris muttered under his breath as we walked out.

Chapter Thirteen

"An optimist says, 'The drink is half-full.' A pessimist says, 'The drink is half-full, but I might have bowel cancer."
—Mr. B., *The Kids in the Hall*

We couldn't find Missi, Louis, or Mom, so we hit poolside, ordering rum from the cabana boys. After a few moments I could feel my blood pressure cooling and remembered something.

"Paris, you ever hear of Doc Savage?"

He rolled his eyes at me. "Not this again! I thought we were done with that, like, thirty years ago."

Bastard. "No. Not the books. Have you heard of anyone else using that name for work?" I launched into an explanation about the guy in my living room. Why hadn't I told him this sooner?

"Huh." Paris leaned back in his chair. "That's a new one. Why was he there?"

"He said he was checking my place out for

Doc Savage." I felt ridiculous even saying it aloud.

"You haven't been made, have you?"

"Either that or the pulp-fiction geeks of the world are after me for some reason." I thought about the last few jobs I'd had. Well, there was that one time I had to take out this drug dealer dressed as Spider-Man at the NYC Comic-Con. He actually tried to shoot a web at me. What a loser. You never bring a webslinger to a gunfight. Nah. That had nothing to do with it. Besides, that was Marvel Comics, not old-fashioned Lester Dent pulp.

"It's probably nothing," Paris said. "We've got more important shit to worry about."

He was right. I was pretty certain the Council would take us up on eliminating the competition.

"How many guys are in that operation?" I asked.

"No one knows." He turned and looked up at the resort. "Okay, maybe they know. It'll be tough. We'll have to work together."

Suddenly my Ralph Lauren preppy look became the soggy Ralph Lauren preppy look as Louis cannonballed into the pool. Missi and Mom sat down to join us.

"He's yours, all right." Missi winked at me.

"Well, of course he is!" Mom snapped. "I

never doubted it for a minute." Good old Mom—she always has my back.

"So, you guys going to come see me later for some stuff?" Missi asked with a giggle.

"You bet your ass I will," I said. "I still have that tricked-out Chia Pet you gave Gin last year."

Monty and Jack, both sixteen, came flying past us and dove into the pool. Monty lifted Louis and threw him through the air until he splash-landed. My son popped above the water, giggling hysterically as Jack tossed him back to Monty. They played with Louis as if he were their own brother. I got a little choked up.

"So, what's next?" Mom asked me, but didn't take her eyes off Louis.

"We meet with Dela in an hour. Looks like we'll get the lowdown on the competition," Paris responded.

Mom nodded. "Great. Then I'm going to take Louis to meet Mother."

I shivered a little, in spite of the heat. "And the tests are, you know, conclusive?"

Missi rolled her eyes. "Well, duh."

An hour later Paris and I found ourselves in Dela's apartment. I have to admit I'd never been in there before. And I was a little nervous that this was where the witch hunt had started against me six months ago.

"We've had our suspicions about National Resources, although your testimony confirmed it today," Dela began. "There are five assassins in the group." She handed us folders. "Each one masquerades as a professional in one industry or another. We don't have photos of them, just some basic info. You will have two weeks to hunt them down."

I opened the folder carefully. *Ugh.* These National Resource guys were real scum. According to the file they took on any contract—regardless of who the vic was. There was a vague reference to the U.S. government—but nothing concrete. A list of their hits told me that they were corporate-motivated, that they'd take out anyone who was giving big business a hard time. Like Erin Brockovich–and Karen Silkwood–type hits. I hated them already. As my blood pressure rose I wondered if they knew who they were killing. At least we Bombays had dossiers on our hits, which were mostly terrorists or really bad criminals. Apparently each of the National Resource assassins had a tattoo on the inside of his forearm of Woody Woodpecker. Weird.

"You'll have to track them down one by one. You can work together. Personally I'd prefer you take them out quickly so word doesn't get out to their colleagues."

"You don't make that easy for us," I said, flipping through the pages. "The only information here seems to be the zip code where each of these guys was last seen." Talk about a needle in a haystack.

"Let me look at that." Paris snatched the files from me. He frowned as he read. "I think I can figure this out. Maybe with some help from Missi."

I threw my hands up in the air. Leave it to him to find the silver lining in a cloud of sludge.

Dela nodded, as if she had known Paris was going to say that. "I'll keep in touch by cell phone, and I expect updates regularly. You two are lucky. Troy wanted to be the handler on this one."

I rolled my eyes. "Great. He hates me."

Dela patted my shoulder. "Don't take it personally, Dakota. He hates everyone."

We thanked Dela and left her apartment, heading for the pool bar. I got a double scotch, and Paris helped himself to a glass of beer. That was another cool perk: free booze. How many companies with high-pressure work offer that? Of course, you wouldn't want cranky assassins when you could placate them with alcohol. Think of any of your family gatherings . . . Thanksgiving, Xmas, you know what I'm talking about. The booze helps.

"You really think we can do this?" I asked after downing my scotch in one swallow. " 'Cause I think we're setting ourselves up for failure."

Paris made a face. "And you used to be such an optimist."

"Well, I'm seriously considering pessimism." I poured myself another glass of scotch. "Optimism is definitely overrated."

"We have everything we need here. The zip codes will narrow things down considerably. Look here." He pointed at the zip code for somewhere in Ohio, then pointed to his laptop. I didn't even realize he'd brought the computer with us. What a geek.

"Tinker, Ohio, has only five thousand people." He pointed to the next one. "And this one's in our own backyard. We can do it."

"How's that? Do you know how long that will take? We don't even know if these are men or women!"

"Why does that matter?" Paris cocked his head at me. "We take them out no matter what."

"I don't know about you, my friend, but I've never taken out a woman before." It's true. And it has nothing to do with scruples. I've just never been assigned a woman. In fact, I don't know if anyone in my family has. Why was that?

"Huh." Paris sat back in his chair. "I haven't either. I wonder why?"

I was getting drunk. "I dunno. Women make lousy terrorists?"

"No. I think they're smarter than that. The only thing women are guilty of is promoting peace." And I could see that he meant it too.

"You've gone soft on me." I scowled. "Women can be just as evil as men."

"Oh, yeah? Name the worst dictators, serial killers, and murderers. They're all men." Paris folded his arms.

I struggled to think. "What about Charlotte Corday? 'Squeaky' Fromme? Sara Jane Moore?"

Paris shook his head. "Those are assassins. They targeted men who they thought were screwing up the world. That doesn't count. I'm looking for women who, just because they were evil, did terrible things to their own."

My brain was getting a little fried. "Oh, screw it. I'm sure they're out there."

Paris looked at me in silence for a moment. "You don't really think much of women, do you?"

Whoa! Where did that come from? "Dude. You're way off. I respect Gin and Liv."

He shook his head. "I'm not talking about family. I'm talking about women in general."

"What the hell?"

"Well, for starters you date only empty-headed blondes. Second, you've never had a serious relationship in your life. And third, you have extreme commitment issues."

I think my draw jopped. I mean jaw dropped. Man, I was drunk. How many drinks did I have? I stared at four wavy highball glasses in front of me—all empty. "That's not true! What about Leonie?"

Paris folded his arms, the smug bastard. "What about Leonie? Are you trying to tell me you respect her?"

"Of course I do!" I sputtered. Paris was now wiggling in front of me like Jell-O. Or at least, that was what I thought I was seeing. If he'd just sit still I could strangle him.

Paris stood up, gathering his things. "Let's face it, Dak: You don't know what respecting a woman means." With that he stood up and walked away.

I was pissed off. But I was too drunk to do anything about it. So I headed up to my room. Mom was watching Louis sleep. When she saw my state of mind she decided to stay with us. I can't blame her. I shouldn't have gotten drunk with my son here. Too late for that. I watched her curl up next to him in his bed and felt an odd pang of regret before I passed out.

I woke up at three thirty a.m., hungover and mad about something without any idea what that was. Paris had something to do with it; I was pretty sure about that. I took off the clothes I'd been sleeping in and, after brushing my teeth and checking to see that Louis and Mom didn't need me for anything, crawled back into bed.

"You look like shit." Missi grinned into the monitor as she buzzed me into the workshop. I didn't know the password. In all honesty I'd never really visited my cousin there before. Paris pushed past me into the room and I followed. I wasn't talking to him. He just didn't know that yet.

"I've felt better." I ran my fingers through my hair. "Do you know about our assignment?"

"Yeah. What can I do to help?"

Paris and I looked at each other. "Well, we were hoping you had a few ideas," Paris said finally.

She cocked her head to the right and said nothing. She was like that sometimes—kind of kooky. Missi would just disappear inside her head for a little while, then emerge with something crazy but perfect.

The workshop was bizarre. I didn't know if she collected this weird shit or was a regular at church bazaars frequented by the mentally ill. I mean, who has a collection of B-list bobble-head dolls? Erik Estrada, Charo, and Alan Alda bobbed and nodded in agreement. *Yeesh.* In the corner was a blast shield. This chick really liked explosives. I remember this one time when she made a toothbrush that blew up when it came into contact with molars—not front teeth, or you may not get the whole head. That kind of work takes a creative thinker. Or a madwoman.

"Well." Missi finally emerged from her thought coma. "I do have a couple of things I can show you." She stood up and we followed her through rows of test tubes, headless Kewpie dolls, remote-controlled lizards, and a poster with a kitten dangling from a branch that said, *Hang in There!*

She stopped in front of a table with a small silver tube. "I did a little research and found out that one of your hits is a zookeeper."

Paris and I exchanged looks before I said, "How did you know that?"

Missi rolled her eyes at us, as if to say, *Hello! Genius here!* "It's the guy in Tinker, Ohio." She tossed us a sheet of paper that did, indeed, have more info on the guy than Dela had given us.

She continued: "The zoo the vic works at has a bear exhibit. I love bears. So unpredictable."

Paris and I looked at each other again. Missi tended to get sidetracked sometimes.

"Anyway"—she pulled herself out of a glazed, faraway look and continued—"like I said, bears are very unpredictable. Especially the smaller black bears. Most people take them for granted because they are little and cute. But use this puppy." She lifted the tube and depressed a button. Clear liquid shot about fifty feet, hitting a stuffed bear (the taxidermied kind) in the face. It didn't look like much, but I thought I detected the strong scent of barbecue sauce. Paris examined the glass-eyed creature. "What does it do?"

Missi rolled her eyes. "This is a highly concentrated mixture of meat essence and bear pheromones. Squirt this on the guy and the bears will charge and tear him limb from limb. Cool, huh?" She lifted the tube to her eye. "And I have it in beef, pork, and chicken flavors. The coroner will just think the zookeeper hit a rib house hard before climbing into the bear pen."

"And we don't have to lay a finger on him. That *is* cool," Paris said as he took the tube from her.

Missi warned, "Don't let it go off here. I got some on my clothes once and a jaguar stalked me for a week." She patted the head of a taxidermied panther. I wondered if she did the work herself.

"Great," I replied, wondering how she had fought and killed the animal. "What else do you have?"

She loaded one of those shopping baskets with two tubes and four vials of the clear liquid. "Okay, this is really cool." We followed her to another part of the room.

She stopped in front of what appeared to be a collection of little porcelain Santa figurines. Was this chick wacky or what?

Missi pulled a Glock .45 with silencer out of a drawer. "This is a gun," she said.

"Wow. Never seen one of those before," I teased. Maybe she was crazier than we all thought.

Missi shook her head. "It's not the gun that's special. It's the ammo." Paris and I watched as she ejected the magazine and slid one of the rounds out. "It's made of gelatin." The bullet was clear, like plastic, with a clear shell casing. She handed us each a bullet. The end was rubbery and the casing was glass. *Huh?*

"I got the idea when I made pineapple Jell-O for the boys. I thought there had to be a way to make a bullet that would cause enough shock trauma to kill a man, but that could also be absorbed by the body so that no bullet would be found."

"Jesus, Missi!" I shouted. "That would revolutionize our industry!"

Paris, more cautious than I was—as usual—agreed. "Yes, it would. But how does it work?"

"It works like a dream." Missi grinned. "Speaking of which, I had the weirdest dream last night. In it, I invented a see-through yarn and knitted a sweater out of it; then I flew to California and ate at the Brown Derby. Everyone thought I was half-naked, which, of course, I wasn't—"

"Um, Missi? The ammo?" I interrupted.

"Oh, yeah." She giggled as if she remembered some joke. "It operates on a similar principle as the icicle maker I did a few years back. Now, you can't really shoot bullets made of ice, because when the gunpowder ignites the gun gets hot and you'd just have a really expensive water gun." She took a deep breath. "And I didn't want to use real Jell-O and have it melt before it entered the body. So I came up with my own mixture that will initially tear into human flesh. Once inside, when it heats up to ninety-eight-point-six degrees, the bullet dissolves—like Jell-O."

"And the casing?" Paris asked as he inspected it.

Missi took the shell from him, popped it into her mouth, and chewed. Before I had a moment to react she stuck out her tongue, showing what appeared to be shards of broken glass.

"Rock candy. Like they make fake glass out of for the movies." Missi grinned and swallowed.

I picked up the pistol. "And this doesn't produce a temperature as high as ninety-eight degrees?"

"Oh, I forgot that part." Missi laughed. "The gelatin takes a couple of minutes to dissolve. It's not in the gun long enough. And I tricked out the silencer with a little cooling system. Kind of like an air conditioner."

I looked at Paris, then turned back to her. "We'll take two and as much ammo as you have."

Missi laughed again and stuffed our basket full. It took her only a few moments to bag everything and send us on our way.

As we headed for the airstrip that night to return home, I couldn't help wondering about my cousin. She was brilliant, but her work would only ever get noticed by the Bombay family. As the plane lifted off the tarmac, I watched the island shrink below me. Now, there was one woman I really respected.

But maybe Paris was right. I had to think

about this Leonie thing. Was I infatuated with her because she was different from the other women I'd been with? Or was it just because she was the only one who could get a rise out of my dick? That was one problem I had to solve.

Mom and Louis enthusiastically regaled us with the story of how Louis met Grandma. My kid went on and on about her collection of souvenirs from all over the world. But I was only half listening. I had a lot to deal with when we got back. But first and foremost on my mind was a smart-assed mortician named Leonie Doubtfire.

Chapter Fourteen

"I am the wild blue yonder. The front line in a never ending battle between good and not so good. Together with my stalwart sidekick, Arthur, and the magnanimous help of some other folks I know, we form the yin to villainy's malevolent yang. Destiny has chosen us. Wicked men, you face the Tick."

—the Tick, *The Tick*

I called Leonie the next day after dropping Louis off at school (where, I might add, he was delirious with delight about the homework he'd have to make up). She sounded happy to hear from me, and we made plans for dinner in two days.

That night Louis and I snuggled up together on the couch with a pizza and watched *Survivor: Gobi Desert*. I love this show. Louis seemed to like it too, as he filled me in on all the geographic information about the area. I just thought it was funny how the producers had run out of tropical locales and were now using a barren wasteland. At least the contestants were back to being scantily clad—

unlike the previous season at the Arctic Circle. Bikinis trumped snowsuits any day, in my book.

"Did you know that the word *Gobi* means desert?" Louis asked me through a mouthful of pizza. He went on to regale me with other odd facts about Mongolia.

"No, I didn't know that." I gave him a squeeze. We were two men (okay, one midget genius and one guy with great hair), bonding over the great American pastime of good pizza and bad television.

Louis and I laughed as the contestants tried to start a fire with no kindling, wood, or matches. Although it did get interesting when some of the women volunteered their T-shirts for the task. That would come back to bite them in the ass when it got really cold that night. *Oh, well.* It's just good fun.

"Dad?" Louis asked me once I tucked him into bed. "I just wanted to say that this has been really overwhelming lately."

Didn't I know it? I grinned. "I know, sport. You've been great about everything."

He looked around the room slowly, before turning back to me. My heart sank, and I had the feeling I was about to be chastised.

"It's just . . ." Louis twisted his hands nervously on his lap, and I realized this was the first time I'd ever seen him like that. "It's just that I don't want to be the grown-up in this relationship . . . like I was with Mom."

My heart skipped the stomach and went straight for my shoes.

"Given the circumstances of my conception," he said.

"Given the circumstances of your conception?" I repeated in shock. "Are you six or forty?"

Louis rolled his eyes, ignoring my comment. "I've been reading your *Maxim* magazines. Anyway, with Mom, she had this scattered life. I had to remind her to pay the bills, take me for checkups, all that stuff. And I'd kind of like to be the kid now."

The room was literally spinning as I tried to absorb what my son had just told me.

"This means," he went on, "no swearing, no drinking too much, and no passing me off to sitters so you can go out."

"Holy shit, Louis!"

He frowned, and I knew I'd already screwed up. It was as if he'd sucker punched me. My first instinct was to be defensive. But how sad is it that I have to defend myself against a six-year-old who is more mature than I am?

"Okay. I'll try." I said, ruffling his hair. "Anything for you."

Louis smiled, and I kissed the top of his head.

Later that night I thought about what he said over and over. And I realized that the kid was right.

Louis and I were really starting to show affection for each other. And to my surprise I discovered that my favorite time of day was picking him up after school. There was a real emotional rush every time he raced out the door and slammed into my arms. I decided the next afternoon that it was time for Leonie and Louis to meet.

"Hey!" Leonie kissed me on the cheek when she answered the door. "Who's this little guy?" I watched carefully to see if she was upset that I had brought a child with me on the date.

Louis extended his right hand, "Louis Torvald-Bombay. Pleased to meet you."

Leonie laughed and shook his hand, shooting me a bemused look. Apparently she was okay with it.

To my surprise Leonie and Louis hit it off immediately. In fact, they talked to each other more than they talked to me. And to my shock I didn't mind. For once all the attention wasn't on me, and yet I felt like everything was perfect. I wanted my new girlfriend to fall in love with my new son.

While they munched on pad thai and chatted about the Gobi Desert (Louis's new obsession), I watched them with fascination. It came as a shock to me that I was witnessing the possible birth of a family. So *this* was what most people did.

A cold sweat crept over me. *Oh, my God.* I was becoming a family man. What happened to me? I used to be perfectly content with my life. Now, in a few short weeks, my life had turned upside down. Panic set in, and for a moment I thought I was going to hyperventilate.

I left Leonie and Louis at the table and headed for the men's room. All of a sudden I needed some space. I found a quiet stall and sat down on the toilet fully clothed.

"'Scuse me." A deep voice interrupted my meditation. "I'm looking for Dakota Bombay."

That was weird. Someone trailed me into the men's room?

"I'll be out in a second." I stood up quietly, sliding my leather belt out of the loops on my Dockers.

The door slammed open, knocking me back against the bowl. I recovered quickly, yanking on my opponent's arm and bringing him to the floor with me. I looped the belt around his neck and twisted.

"What the hell, man?" I asked the gurgling man in my grip, "What do you want with me?"

"Some guy sent me," he rasped, struggling

to get his fingers between the leather and his skin.

"Who?" I tightened my grip on his throat.

"Doc Savage . . ."

I almost dropped my belt. Again? I thought for a few moments about what I should ask next.

"What did Doc Savage want you to do?" I growled in his ear.

Shit. He was unconscious. I watched as his body dropped to the floor. Now what? After slipping my belt back on I made sure the bathroom door was locked. Working quickly, I sat him on a toilet in one of the stalls, pulling his pants down to his ankles and leaning him back against the wall. I crawled under the door so it would stay closed and cleaned myself up in the mirror. That's one of the things I like about strangulation: It's not very messy, and you don't have to actually kill them. It's all about the pressure.

No one would notice him, and by the time he woke up we'd be long gone. I just had to make sure I paid with cash instead of a credit card and no one would know I was even there.

"Who wants ice cream?" I announced when I made it back to the table. Louis started jumping up and down in his seat and Leonie smiled, so I guess that was a yes. I paid the bill and the three of us climbed into my car and headed for Whitey's, best damn ice cream in the Midwest.

"I like you," Leonie said to me with a wink as we sat outside eating.

"Wow. I'm honored," I responded. Louis ignored us both, intent on inhaling his ice cream.

She laughed. It was a wonderful sound. Maybe the perfect sound. *Huh.* I always used to think the perfect sound came from a blonde moaning with pleasure.

"I mean it," she answered.

"I like you, too." *Wow.* This conversation was going nowhere. Then why did I feel so good?

"Dad thinks you're cool," Louis said through an ice-cream goatee and mustache.

"Louis!" Was I . . . was I *blushing*?

My son nodded. "It's true. I think he's quite taken with you."

Leonie smiled at me, then leaned down to Louis. "You know what? I really like him too."

"Why?" I asked before I realized it was a strange question. I mean, I knew why I liked her. But I needed to know why she liked me. For most of my life I just took it for granted that chicks dug me. *Huh.* I guess I never really cared what it was about me they liked. And yet, it seemed very important for me to know what Leonie saw in me.

"I guess it's because you're funny, and weird. You don't act around me like I think you usually act around women."

"What? I'm weird? Really?" *Wow*. Didn't see that one coming.

Leonie grinned. "Somehow I feel that I'm the first woman to see who you really are. The first one to see your vulnerable side, maybe. Everything else seems like an act. But around me you're tongue-tied. That's a major turn-on."

Oh, my God. She liked me when I acted like a geek? What the hell? That wasn't what women wanted! They wanted handsome and confident men. Alpha males. Right? Wasn't that right? Vulnerable? Was she bullshitting me?

Leonie pulled a napkin out of her pocket and giggled as she wiped the ice cream off Louis's face. She looked so natural doing that. Her mass of red hair tickled the boy's cheek and he laughed, and I realized that Louis and Leonie belonged together. The question was, where did I fit into the picture?

Chapter Fifteen

[Szell prepares to torture Babe a second time] "Oh, don't worry. I'm not going into that cavity. That nerve's already dying. A live, freshly cut nerve is infinitely more sensitive. So I'll just drill into a healthy tooth until I reach the pulp. That is unless, of course, you can tell me that it's safe."

—Christian Szell, *Marathon Man*

"Don't forget about our little appointment!" Gin's voice bubbled on the answering machine when Louis and I got home. *Damn.* I forgot about that. Diego was accompanying Romi's class on a field trip, so I'd promised a month ago to take Gin to her appointment with a dental surgeon.

Taking Gin to get her wisdom teeth out was the last thing I wanted to do. But in the Bombay family we had to use the buddy system anytime we would be under anesthesia.

"Are you sure you want him in here?" Dr. Munch asked my sister. He looked a little concerned about my presence. I could understand that. If he screwed up, he wouldn't want a witness. But rules are rules. It only had to happen once, and it happened to my great-great-great-uncle Francisco. He went in to get his gallstones out and, while under the influence, started talking about killing the mayor of Montevideo with a fish fork. Fortunately the doctor thought he was just hallucinating and had no idea that the year before, the mayor of Montevideo had, in fact, bought it with a fish fork in a kind of creative tracheotomy, shall we say. Since then . . . well, we kind of borrowed the buddy system from the Boy Scouts.

"Sorry, Doctor," Gin said, "but I'm too nervous without my brother here for moral support. You understand." Of course, my sister isn't afraid of anything. In fact, she could probably pull her own teeth. Maybe we should consider having a dentist in the family.

The dental surgeon reluctantly agreed, then, after casting me a sidelong glance, proceeded to shoot my sister full of Novocain.

"You'll feel a pinch," he said as he plunged the needle into the roof of her mouth.

Yeah, right. A pinch. We practically had to peel Gin off the ceiling after that pinch. After three more shots on both sides, the doctor left.

"You okay?" I asked cautiously. Gin looked like she'd had a stroke.

"Thith feelth weird," she slurred. Her cheeks had collapsed into jowls.

I, of course, started to laugh.

"Ith noth funny!" She turned red, and I laughed harder.

"It's just, you're usually such a talker!" I wiped a few tears away. "And now you can't! This is too good!"

"Athhole." Gin crossed her arms over her chest.

After a few minutes the doctor came back in. "Are you numb?" he asked Gin.

She nodded after slapping both cheeks. "Yeth. Thee?"

Dr. Munch nodded and picked up a tool I suspect was frequently used during the Spanish Inquisition.

"You won't feel any pain, but you will feel pressure, and you'll hear cracking and popping as I pull the tooth out." Without waiting for her to respond, he reached into her mouth and wrestled with the firmly wedged tooth.

I was fascinated. I'd only been on the receiving end before. The doc was a large man, but he practically had to put his knee on Gin's chest to loosen up the tooth. Finally he pulled the bloody mess out. I watched with awe as he did the same thing on the other side.

My cell went off and I saw it was a text

from Paris. Turning my back on Gin, I flipped open the phone.

First target—Norbert Munch, DDS. Last kill—whistle-blower for Halliburton.

I blinked. This couldn't be happening. I felt like I was in a trance as I closed the phone and turned back to Gin.

"There you go, all done." And then Dr. Norbert E. Munch rolled up his sleeves.

I froze. Woody Woodpecker mocked me from his inner wrist. It was the tattoo of the National Resources assassins. *Holy shit!* I didn't think it would be this easy. I mean, I knew one of them was a local—but what were the odds?

Unfortunately the dentist/assassin saw that I saw. I jumped for the door to block his escape. He charged and I threw him to the floor, where we wrestled silently on the linoleum. The man grabbed my testicles and squeezed—an act of war, as far as I was concerned. Pain flooded my line of vision, and I bit my tongue so I wouldn't scream. Of course, then my tongue hurt too. My hand reached the tray above us, and I found a long-handled dental mirror.

My assailant flipped me into a submission hold. This guy was good. So good that my vision was starting to blur. I could feel myself losing consciousness, so I took the only chance I had and plunged the end of the mirror deep into his eye socket. His hold relaxed, and I scrambled to my feet as he flopped around on the floor.

"You killed my denthal thurgeon?" Gin asked woozily. *Oops.* I forgot about her.

I nodded. "Council assignment. I only just got his name, but I had to take him out."

"Well, thath jutht fantathtic." Gin rolled her eyes. "How the hell are we going to deal with thith? The nurth will be in any moment!"

I hadn't thought of that. Bombays never left behind a body if it could implicate them. And this sure seemed to be that situation. It would be tough to leave him in here when Gin was listed as the last patient he had before he died.

Think, Dak! Gin looked like a deranged chipmunk with her cheeks stuffed with gauze. She wouldn't be a lot of help. *Great.*

The building was designed like a bunker: low-slung, one story, with high, narrow windows. I squinted, wondering if I could pass the body through it. Of course, it was getting close to rush hour, and we were facing a street with a lot of traffic. No, that wouldn't look suspicious at all.

We'd run out of time. If they didn't have Gin's name, address, and insurance provider, I'd just stuff the doctor in the closet and run for it. But it wouldn't take long for them to notice he wasn't anywhere in the building. They'd find him, and Gin would be a suspect. I didn't feel like busting her out of the police department à la Terminator, so I had to come up with something else . . . and quickly.

I started screaming like a little girl (mainly due to the fact that my testicles had just been crushed). "Oh, my God! Doctor! Somebody call 911!"

Gin narrowed her eyes at me, then rolled them. Okay, so it wasn't much of a plan, but I needed her compliance.

"Thocther Munth? Thocther Munth?" She knelt down beside the body, which I turned facedown. After shooting me a pissed-off look, she continued: "I think he'th dead!"

Two nurses and another surgeon ran into the room and stopped when they saw their colleague facedown on the stick end of a dental mirror.

We had to stay there for three hours while the police (or "poleeth," as Gin called them) and coroner came to investigate. At one point I think the Novocain wore off and Gin was in desperate need of painkillers, because she fainted. Somehow we managed to convince everyone that the doctor was walking with the implement in his hand when he slipped on a little puddle of Gin's drool (I made that part up just for fun—Gin didn't like it much, because when everyone's back was turned she had to spit on the floor) and fell onto his mirror.

"Happens all the time," the bored coroner said to me. "You wouldn't believe how many people die in freak accidents."

Actually, he'd be surprised to know how many "freak accidents" were really Bombay family hits. But I wasn't about to tell him that.

"You bastard!" Gin lit into me once I got her back home. "What if I get dry sockets? I can't ever go back there, you know!"

I ran my hands through my hair. "I said I was sorry! I didn't expect him to be the one." We were talking in code because the kids were in the next room. Diego finished making an ice pack for his wife and handed it to her in silence. I knew he was uncomfortable with our livelihood. But he didn't argue either.

I took out my cell phone and dialed Paris. "Got one. Four more to go."

"I found number two, "he said." We're going to Indianapolis tomorrow." He clicked off.

Chapter Sixteen

"The first rule of Fight Club is, you do not talk about Fight Club. The second rule of Fight Club is, you *do not* talk about Fight Club. . . . And the final rule: if this is your first night at Fight Club, you have to fight."
　　　　　　　　—Tyler Durden, *Fight Club*

"Are you sure this is him?" I whispered. We had fifth-row seats to a motivational business seminar in Indy. Paris had bought our tickets online under assumed names, and we were wearing wigs, cheap suits, and large, plastic-framed glasses.

"Yup."

My cousin had hacked into the reservations and got us into the ten-thousand-strong business seminar as Mr. Tom Olds and Mr. James Smith. Apparently we were salesmen for Massengill. Yeah, I was excited about that too.

Anthony Lowe had taken the stage, pacing back and forth as he shouted lame encouragements and vague success strategies.

"And with my one-hundred-percent-foolproof plan, you can triple your sales in the next six months . . . guaranteed!" He went on to share several situations where this worked, but to me it sounded as if he were telling the stories of Sam Walton and Bill Gates—just leaving out their names. Lowe went on to plug his ten-CD collection that usually sold for $500. We could get it for $399 today only, cash and credit cards accepted.

I really hated this guy. But I was starting to hate the audience more for believing this shit. We'd been there for three hours already, and I've got to be honest with you: I still didn't have any idea how to sell douche bags more effectively. All he offered was a bunch of clichés, promising that if you bought his CDs you could achieve nirvana, win salesman of the year, and find yourself wealthy with a knockout trophy wife. What a rip-off artist.

Finally a break in the seminar found us in the cement hallways around the auditorium, dining on greasy hot dogs and stale nachos.

"Isn't he brilliant?" A mousy woman in a flower-patterned dress sighed aloud to the tall, thin man next to her.

"Tomorrow," the man said while nodding, "he's going to zip-line onto the stage. That'll be cool."

I raised my eyebrows at Paris and he nodded, indicating that he'd heard it too. We tuned out the stupid couple (turns out they sold insurance) and moved on. As the crowd started to reenter the auditorium, Paris and I slipped around to the backstage area.

"James Smith," I shouted as I stuck out my right hand to the harried-looking teenager with a clipboard. "I was told that my colleague and I won a backstage tour." Paris nodded, pushing his glasses up on his nose.

"Oh! Um, really?" The girl looked as if she were wound pretty tight. "I didn't, uh, know. Okay." She flipped through the papers on the clipboard, but found nothing indicating that two Massengill salesmen had won such a precious commodity.

Fortunately for us, an even more mentally-challenged kid walked by.

"Ernie!" the girl shouted. "These guys get a backstage tour!" Then with a nod toward Ernie she walked away, presumably proud of herself.

Ernie squinted at us. He was tall and skinny, with a pronounced slouch and blue hair. He wiped his nose on the sleeve of a shirt that was way too big for him. His tie had an eagle on it with the words, *I'm a Winner*, in gilt script.

"Okay." He sniffled. "Let's get this over with."

Apparently Ernie wasn't caught up in the excitement of the show. He looked like he'd hire us to hit himself if he had to do one more day here.

"This is the green room, where the celebrities wait until they go onstage." Ernie pointed to a closed door. Celebrities? What, was he kidding? "And that's the staff lounge. We got Fruit Roll-Ups and juice boxes in there."

I closed my eyes in an attempt to avoid strangling Ernie with his tie.

He led us past vending machines, which he pointed out to us as if we had never seen one before, and light and sound techs who were drinking some mystery liquid from bottles wrapped in brown paper, to the exit doors, and finally to the backstage area.

We stood there, watching from the wings as Anthony spun bullshit into gold. Gold that would, at the end of the day, go only into his pockets. My guess was that our tour guide barely made minimum wage. It didn't look like Ernie could afford clothes that fit.

"We heard Mr. Lowe is riding a zip line to the stage tomorrow." Paris pushed his glasses up again. "Is that true?"

I looked at Ernie, who sighed heavily. "Yeah. He's been wanting to do it for a long time. This is the only place the techies think it's possible." I followed the line of his arm as he pointed to a catwalk in the wings.

"He'll go from there, offstage"—he slowly led his index finger down toward the stage— "to center stage. I'm not really sure why he's doing it, but oh, well."

A crash came from right behind us, and we watched as Ernie scrambled in its direction. He'd already forgotten our existence, which was good, since we'd have to kill him otherwise.

Back in our seats Paris whispered, "We'll have to come in tonight and weaken it somehow. Maybe shred some of the cable."

I heard some laughter to my left. It distracted me only for a moment before I leaned in and answered, "Maybe we could take the steel out of the pulley, replace it with plastic or something else that would fall apart quickly." However we did it, I really wanted this idiot to die dramatically. A humiliating death is so much more fun when it happens to an asshole.

The laughter came again, and I turned toward it. Sitting to my left were two burly good ol' boys. You know the kind. The ones who are trapped in the 1950s and still pinch their secretary's ass for fun. The kind who think if a woman isn't interested in them, she's a lesbian. The kind who take their wedding rings off when they travel out of town for business.

"Is there a problem?" I asked. Paris punched me in the arm. I know, I know: Maintain a low profile at all times. But this bullshit seminar was killing me.

"Now that you mention it, son," the larger of the two answered, "I was just wondering what a couple of dandies like you sell?"

Dandies? Are you kidding me? I looked at my polyester suit. It was far more obvious that we resembled seventies porn actors! And who the hell said *dandies* anymore? *Thanks, Paris. Next time I'll pick the disguises.*

"I b'lieve my colleague asked you a question," the lesser of the two fat men said. "What do you sell?"

"Oh, I don't know if you two boys can handle it," I replied slowly, ignoring the repeated punches from Paris.

"That's funny, son." Son? Were we on *The Dukes of Hazzard*? "But what business are you in?" They looked pissed off.

Never one to shrink from a challenge, I leaned forward and looked carefully from side to side. Paris started kicking me, but I wasn't about to stop. "Lobster semen."

"What?" The one closest to me looked as if his eyes were going to pop.

I brought my index finger to my lips. "Shhh! We aren't supposed to tell anyone."

"Boy, are you trying to tell me you sell lobster jizz?" the big one asked.

I nodded. "There's big money in that. Those of us in the business call it white gold." I added a wink for emphasis.

"I don't believe you," the smaller one said, folding his arms across his chest.

I leaned back in my seat. "I don't care if you believe me. But my wife does, every time we visit our oceanfront home in Jamaica, and every time she has the Bentley washed." I would've gone on and on, but what was the point? I still didn't know why I came up with lobster semen.

"You make good commissions on that?" Big One asked, his eyes the size of salad plates.

I nodded. "About thirty grand on the East Coast, twenty thousand in the panhandle, forty K in California. Throw in the rest of the country, and we're talking close to a quarter mil. Breeders are begging for this stuff."

Paris coughed, trying to get my attention, but I was too far gone.

"Our client supplies the seed of giant blue lobsters. We can't keep up with the orders."

"How do we know you're not havin' fun

with us?" Little Fat Man broke in, a bit disgruntled about the whole thing.

"Well, let me put it to you this way: You go into any grocery store here in Indianapolis and you'll see a tank of live lobsters, right?"

Both men nodded.

I continued, "Indiana is a landlocked state. You think about the hundreds of thousands of stores in this great country of ours, and you know in your heart there aren't that many lobsters in both oceans to keep up with supply. That's why there are breeders!" I sat back, looking smug. Paris snickered in spite of himself.

"How can a couple of guys like us get in on this action?" One of them leaned toward me conspiratorially.

I acted as if I were thinking about it. Then Paris whispered in my ear (he said, "You're an idiot," but that's beside the point), and I nodded.

"I'll tell you what." I pointed at the stage. "Mr. Lowe got us into it about five years ago. Now, you go up to him after the show tonight and ask him about it. He'll deny it, and he's supposed to. But if you're really persistent, he'll relent and give you the info." I leaned back in my chair. "Then when we see you boys here next year, we can compare the size of the diamonds we buy for our wives."

The fat men laughed knowingly. Paris and I slipped away at the next break. Sure, I was having a good time, but there was still work to do.

It didn't take us long to find a couple of backstage passes (you'd be surprised how many people just leave those things lying around) and to question a completely stoned technician about who would be there that night, when did they lock up, etc.

I loved sneaking around backstage. The passes worked like a charm. The staff members were few and far between, and it was dark enough that we could hide if needed. After about half an hour of this, Paris and I swiped a detailed schedule (again, just lying around), then headed back to the hotel.

"We should go back at midnight," Paris said after a shower. I couldn't blame him. Those clothes were hot and scratchy.

I nodded. "Sure. But this time we dress my way." Tomorrow we'd have to put on the cheap suits again, but tonight it would be black cashmere. I had it imported. Pure, one hundred percent Mongolian cashmere. It would be like wearing silk pajamas to a break-in.

So, sure enough, we found ourselves back at the arena at twelve eleven. Okay, we were a little late, but I'd really wanted some nachos. I think I got a secondhand pot buzz from the roadie earlier.

We managed to slip inside before the last of the staff called it a night. According to the stoner, the building was open all night and had security guards twenty-four/seven. No problem. My experience has been that these guys usually find a nice warm closet and bed down for the night.

By twelve forty-five a.m. we were alone backstage trying to decide what would work better, weakening the cable or screwing up the pulley. One rock-paper-scissors game later, we were working on Paris's plan to weaken the cable. How was I supposed to know the bastard would pick paper? He usually picks scissors and I usually pick rock. Oh. Maybe he knew that. I hate it when I find out I'm not as smart as I thought I was.

While Paris worked on fraying the cable, I replaced the steel carabiners with cheap aluminum ones and significantly loosened the screws that held the cable in place. We wanted it to look like an accident, like human error and equipment malfunction. I could live with that. If none of the above worked, there was always one of Missi's transparent bullets.

Once we were satisfied, we slipped past the snoozing guard at the door and made it back to the hotel. Paris dropped off immediately, but I wanted to do some work on my wig. It was so crappy that no matter what I did, it continued to resume its ugly bowl shape. Damn synthetic hair.

Louis popped into my head once I stretched out. I was surprised to notice that I smiled automatically. Damn, he was cute. How did I end up with a kid like that? I felt bad that I didn't remember his mom. I would've liked to have known more about the mother of my son.

A shock of pain hit my stomach, and I realized I felt bad that I'd treated her like all the other women. Whoever she was, she did a good job raising Louis. And I was depressed that I couldn't thank her for that.

Chapter Seventeen

Vesper Lynd: "It doesn't bother you; killing all those people?"

James Bond: "Well, I wouldn't be very good at my job if it did."

—*Casino Royale*

The next morning, at nine a.m. sharp, Paris and I (incognito again in the seventies-porn-flunky look) stood in the doorway of the auditorium closest to the backstage area. Why weren't we in our seats? Well, one reason was to avoid the rednecks who sat next to us yesterday (I smiled, thinking of them pestering Lowe about lobster semen all night), and the other was that if something went wrong with the hit, we could finish off the target quickly.

"I've been thinking about what you said," I whispered to Paris.

"Hmmm?" He was busy studying his watch. Lowe's lethal zip-line moment was about to make motivational-speaker history.

"What you said about women. How I don't seem to respect them."

Paris arched his right eyebrow. "We're working now. Can't this wait?"

I nodded, then went on anyway. "I was just thinking about Louis's mom. How I don't even remember her. And I think you're right about me."

"That's great, Dak. This is a real break-through for you, but the wrong time." Okay, he sounded pissed.

I turned my eyes to the stage. *Damn.* They were running late. After scanning the audience I thought about talking to Paris again, but something in his posture dissuaded me.

Music started up, you know, the kind of dun-dun-dee-dun thingy that announces the arrival of the king, dictator, sheikh, whatever.

"Do you want to zip through success?" Anthony Lowe's voice came from backstage. The crowd went wild. I rolled my eyes, thinking, *Just die already.*

"Then follow me!" Lowe screamed, and the audience screamed.

Paris and I watched as Lowe started to appear at the side of the stage, about forty feet off the floor. As if on cue the cable gave way, dumping the speaker unceremoniously in a heap on the right side of the stage. That was a serious drop. But people have been known to survive high falls, so I held my breath. The crowd was unnervingly silent. For once in his life, I realized, Mr. Lowe had the complete attention of everyone in the room. *How nice.*

We waited just a few more minutes for the stagehands to do the typical, "Oh, my God, he's dead," and the expected gasp from the audience, before Paris and I headed for the exits.

"I just wanted you to know that you were right," I started up as we walked out to the parking lot.

Paris stopped and looked at me. "What are you talking about?"

I explained to him that I was up pretty late thinking about Louis's mom, how I felt like an asshole for how I had most likely treated her. We continued on to the car and got in. Paris listened quietly.

"That's great, Dak." He finally spoke as we got into the car. "I never thought you'd come around."

"And I wanted you to be the first to know. And as soon as we get back I'm going to invite the family to a barbecue at Gin's house to meet Leonie."

"Why at Gin's house?" Paris asked.

"Well, duh! Gin has a backyard and a grill. I don't." It made sense to me.

* * *

Gin was more than enthusiastic to host the family. Diego nodded and winked. Mom screamed into the phone when I invited her and Dad, and Liv was so excited that she spoke in a shrill, high-pitched voice that I believe only chipmunks could understand.

Apparently I'd never done this before. I didn't realize I'd never brought a woman home to meet the family. I called Leonie and she sounded amused, but agreed.

"That's awesome, Dad!" Louis howled when I told him.

"Really?" I asked him.

He nodded. "Yeah! All my cousins—Romi, Alta, and Woody—will be there! My whole family! I never got to do stuff like this when Mom was alive. She avoided her family."

I thought about what he said for a moment before responding. "Louis? I'm really sorry I didn't know your mom that well. I wish I had."

My son arched his right eyebrow. "Really? She told me the same thing once. That she wished she'd gotten to know you better."

That kind of stunned me. "Oh. I didn't know that." I cleared my throat. "Are you mad at me?"

His eyes grew wide. "No. Why would I be?"

I shrugged and picked at a piece of the carpet with the toe of my shoe. Louis made me feel as if *I* were the six-year-old.

"I don't know. I just wanted you to know that . . . well . . . I love you, and I'm glad you're here."

Louis flew into my arms, crushing me with his embrace. "I love you too, Dad," came the muffled reply.

I set him down, trying discreetly to brush away a tear as I did so. "So, you like the Bombay family?" I tried to change the subject. My heart was beating so violently I thought I was having a heart attack.

"Oh, yeah! My cousins are cool, and I love Grandma and Grandpa! Paris and Missi are a lot of fun to talk to, and Gin and Liv are like having two moms! Although I do think it's weird no one in this family seems to have a day job. But after this trip to Santa Muerta, I figure we're all independently wealthy."

Maybe this would've been the right time to tell him what the Bombay family business was. Romi and Alta had started their training last year. And Woody was four years away from his first kill. They all knew.

But something held me back. Louis was a genius. He wouldn't just take the information and live with it. Chances were my kid would analyze it—bring up the ethical questions most of us spent our whole lives avoiding. It was a pretty safe bet to think that Louis would not join us without a fight. I'd have to do something I'd never done before—prepare. Make sure I had good reasons for what we do. Maybe I should talk to Liv and Gin about it.

So, I changed the subject and we spent the afternoon planning the party. Louis chose hot dogs, hamburgers, and a decorated cake depicting the wonders of the Gobi Desert. I'm not kidding.

On a Saturday afternoon my family stood in a semicircle in Gin's backyard, ready to meet Leonie. I made my introductions, and Leonie laughed. The Bombay family rushed to mob her, and I realized everything was going to be okay.

"Wow, Dak." Gin sat down next to me at the picnic table. "She's amazing. I'm kind of in shock." She took a drink from her bottle of beer and winked at me.

I watched as Liv, Mom, and Leonie talked animatedly a few yards away. "I guess I've never brought anyone home to meet the family before."

"And this one has a brain. Very cool," Gin said.

I punched my sister in the arm. "Are you saying I didn't date intelligent women before?"

"With the exception of Louis's mom, yes." Gin motioned toward my son, who was seriously engaged in a water-gun fight with his cousins, Diego, Paris, and Liv's husband, Todd. It felt so . . . so suburban.

"Missi ran the DNA test on Louis. He is my son; I think I can claim some of that intelligence."

"No, little brother. It definitely didn't come from you. I think he gets it from me."

I gave her my best evil eye as Liv joined us. "I have a son. How cool is he?"

"He's amazing!" Liv gushed. "And Leonie's great too. Hell has definitely frozen over today."

"Oh, come on!" I protested. "You had to know that this might happen someday!"

My sister and cousin shook their heads simultaneously. Gin said, "You are growing up." Liv added insult to injury by nodding in agreement.

I focused on Leonie as she chatted happily with Mom and Dad. She was nothing like any woman I'd dated before. I knew she was special, and we hadn't even slept together yet. Hell, we haven't really even made out! The old Dak would be panicking right now. But I wasn't the old Dak, was I?

What was it about her that invaded my

thoughts day and night? She was smart, funny, and didn't put up with my bullshit. I should *hate* that in a woman. But Leonie Doubtfire was different. She was like a best friend.

Huh? It startled me to think of a woman as a buddy. That was impossible. And if she were a friend, I wouldn't be attracted to her. And yet I was.

"Hey, Gin," I started, "can Louis spend the night?"

"Of course. Why?"

I shuffled my feet under the table, then ran my fingers through my hair. "I think tonight's the night with Leonie." I couldn't believe I'd just said that. In fact, it looked like Gin and Liv couldn't believe it either, by the way their jaws hung open.

"What are you saying?" Gin asked.

I could feel a blush coming on. This was completely alien to me. "It means what it means."

Liv looked from me to Gin, then back to me. "You mean you two haven't . . ."

"You and Leonie haven't slept together yet?" Gin finished.

I nodded. They fainted. Okay, so I'm just making that part up. But judging by their reactions, that's what should've happened. I guess I could understand that. They'd known me as a player since I was sixteen. Hell, I still couldn't believe it.

Liv, normally a wine drinker, opened a bottle of beer and chugged it. *Wow.* I'd never seen her do that before. Gin couldn't stop staring at me. Apparently they were in shock. Problem was, so was I.

When the cookout ended I led Leonie through the receiving line of well-wishers and out to my car. She didn't ask where we were going, and I was so excited I don't think I could've answered her. I was pretty sure I was going to get laid. No, scratch that. I was going to make love to Leonie. I was going to make love perhaps for the first time ever. And I was scared shitless.

Chapter Eighteen

"An assassin without confidence is a horrible thing to behold. It's like a relief pitcher who fumbles the ball."

—Julian Noble, *The Matador*

Man, I was completely messed up. My hands were shaking, my heart was pounding, and for a moment I flirted with the idea of dropping everything to see a neurologist. I had trouble getting the key into the lock.

I felt like Chevy Chase playing Gerald Ford. Upon entering the condo I became a stumbling oaf. I tripped on the hall rug, smashing a small table in the process. I left it where it lay, a splintered casualty of my nerves. Apparently my brain was not sending the right messages to my arms and legs. I skidded down the hallway to the living room, wondering if an unknown assailant had broken in and recklessly waxed my floor. I led her to the sofa, and fortunately Leonie wisely ignored it when I fell backward over the hassock.

Somehow I managed to sit on the couch without impaling myself on the sculpture next to it. When I ran my fingers through Leonie's hair, the dark red strands knotted around my ring. I started to pull my hand away, only to have her cry out in pain. This was going so well. Were Gin and Paris watching me on a planted video camera right now? I wouldn't put it past them.

As I leaned toward her (forcing my sister and best friend from my thoughts), my right hand still stuck in her hair, we actually hit our front teeth together. Somehow her lip was caught in the middle, and as I pulled away I could see I'd given her a fat lip. And who the hell turned up my thermostat?

In spite of all of this (and I know this will sound weird), I was really turned on. Just looking at Leonie, smelling her hair, touching her skin, sent shivers to all the appropriate body parts. I wanted her so badly my stomach hurt.

I pulled back for a moment. "Why are you here?"

She laughed. "Well, for starters, you invited me. And I wanted to come over."

"Why?" I persisted. Suddenly I had to know why this amazing woman was interested in me. Wait a minute. I never cared about that before! But for some reason, with Leonie I did.

"What do you mean, why?"

"I just wanted to know why you picked me," I said.

Leonie studied me for a moment. "Somehow I get the impression you never asked anyone that before." When all I did was shrug, she continued: "There's something about you, Dak. I'm very attracted to you."

"Why?" *Dammit!* What the hell was wrong with me? It was like having an out-of-body experience—one where I couldn't stop myself if I wanted to.

For a moment I thought I'd pushed her too far. Maybe if she thought about it too much she'd realize she wasn't attracted to me. What had I done?

"I find your vulnerability endearing," she said quietly, with a smile. "I love how you get tongue-tied around me, as if I were the first woman to do that to you. You make me feel like I'm the most desirable person in the world."

For a moment—just a moment—I thought she was insulting me. Vulnerable? Tongue-tied? That wasn't me! I was suave and worldly. Did this mean she didn't see that?

"Dak." Leonie pulled me against her. "I want you. Don't ruin it."

Leonie's lips were soft on mine. All of a sudden I forgot what to do! A sense of panic hit me, and it felt as if the room were spinning. She seemed calm. What the hell was wrong with me? Maybe I needed to lie down.

"Why don't we take this into the bedroom?" Leonie whispered in my ear. I did one of those cartoon gulps and nodded. We walked into what had once been my playboy lair. Now it seemed like an alien room with furniture I didn't even recognize.

Leonie kissed me, then abandoned me to use the bathroom. I stood there, frozen to the spot where she had left me, unable to think of what to do. *Shit!* This had never happened to me before! *Think, Dak, think!*

I was still standing there when Leonie returned and wrapped her long arms around me, pulling me into a kiss. I'm not certain how she managed that, since my head was spinning on my neck like a top. What was it with this chick? I was completely messed up!

What happened next was a blur. There was a whole host of sensations involving hands, fingers, lips, and tongues. The outside of my body was performing, but my innards felt like the inside of a Lava lamp. I barely remember our clothes coming off, or slipping beneath the sheets. All I could see were those hypnotic light blue eyes framed by a cloud of silky red curls. I hoped she'd know what to do. I'd forgotten what happened when

you got a naked man and a naked woman together.

Leonie guided my body into hers, and I felt
a surge of crushing emotion. What was
this? It was as if all my organs had swollen
up with helium, and I was about to take
flight.

Oh, my God. I had to stop this. I had to
channel George Clooney instead of Woody
Allen. That very idea turned it around.

I started to take control of the situation,
like I used to. I kissed her lips, then her chin,
slipping down to the lovely hollow of her long,
pale throat. Leonie sighed, and I became
bolder. I wanted to make this night memorable, not come across as a bungling fool.

My lips sought the cleft between her perfect, small breasts, and I nuzzled each nipple
until she moaned beneath me. It felt so good
to make her feel good—something I'd never
noticed before. Cupping her shapely ass, I
found her sweet spot. It took only a few moments to make her come, and it was so good
for her, it felt like I'd climaxed too.

Leonie flipped me over, climbing on top,
and once I was inside her she began to rock
back and forth, never taking her eyes off of
mine. I winced as I realized I'd never thought
of my past lovers as people. Shoving that
aside, I closed my eyes against the intensity

of her gaze before my orgasm washed over me like a tidal wave.

I felt so terrified and wonderful, I started to cry. Yup. You heard me.

The more I tried to stop the faster the tears came. I lay there on my back, arms around Leonie—whose hair covered my chest—and wept. The intensity of what happened stunned me. And I didn't know what the hell to do.

Fortunately Leonie fell asleep and I just lay there, wondering what the hell was happening.

The deep, homey tang of bacon teased me awake. I was naked and alone in bed, but someone was making breakfast. This I understood—recognizing the smell of meat and knowing that a woman was here.

I reached for my robe, but it was gone. After fumbling in my drawers for pajamas, I wandered into the hall toward the kitchen.

"Morning!" Leonie called out brightly as she flipped the eggs and bacon simmering in front of her. My robe hung from her slight frame, but it looked incredibly beautiful against her pale skin. She resembled a china doll dressed up in silk.

"Hey." I kissed her awkwardly and poured a cup of coffee. "How long have you been up?"

I've never been good at the morning-after

thing. In fact, unless there was an opportunity for follow-up sex, I usually rushed them through the shower and out the door so I could get on with the next conquest. But this morning was different. This morning I wanted her to stay.

"Not long. I was hungry. I hope you don't mind." She pushed a spiral strand of copper curls from her forehead.

"Of course not. I love having you here." *Oh, my God.* It was true. I wanted her here for more than sex! Well, that and she was making bacon. Show me a man who'd turn that down.

"Your family is amazing," Leonie said as she brought two plates to the table and sat down to eat. "Especially Louis."

I grinned. "Yeah. He's pretty adorable."

"I love your sister and cousin. Gin? And Liv? Is her name really Gin Bombay?" She giggled, giving me goose bumps.

"It's really Virginia or Ginny. But we pretty much shortened it to Gin over the years. It's much funnier that way."

Leonie paused, holding her coffee cup. "I have a question that I hope doesn't offend you." She waited for me to nod before continuing. "It's just that I noticed you introduced Gin's husband as Diego Bombay. Isn't that your name too?"

Well, at least she didn't say anything about

the dagger-throwing competition at the barbecue, or ask why there's a huge keypad in the kitchen locking up Gin's basement. This was one of the Bombay family quirks I could clue her in on.

"It's a weird little requirement in my family. If you marry a Bombay woman you have to take her name. It's been that way since 2000 BCE. None of the men seem to mind." I shrugged. "I guess I never really thought about it before."

Leonie held my gaze for a moment. "Well, I think it's really cool. Apparently your family is more progressive than most."

Yeah. We were progressive, all right. As long as if what you mean by progressive was that we kill people we don't know for money. "So, you got along with everyone?" That was a weird question. As if I were interviewing her for a job.

"I did. They are really terrific. You are so lucky."

I sat back as she took a few bites of her breakfast. I guess she was right. I usually did think I was lucky to be born rich and unfairly attractive. I just never associated the word *luck* with my family before.

"And your son, Louis, I adore him!" Leonie giggled. "I've never met a kid like that before."

"Yeah. If it weren't for the DNA test, I'd think he wasn't related to me at all." *Oops*.

Leonie arched her right eyebrow. "DNA test?" Uh-oh.

I sighed and told her about my short acquaintance with my son. For some reason I told her everything, warts and all. I didn't even try to make myself sound better. I made a mental note to make an appointment with a neurologist tomorrow.

"Wow," she said softly. "That's a lot for a little kid to handle."

I nodded and realized that, for once in my life, I was agreeing with her instead of saying, *What about me? It was tough for me too!*

"And the family made you take the test? That's pretty cold."

"Well, it's really my grandmother who pushed for it. I did it just to keep her happy. I knew Louis was mine." Or at least, I wanted to believe Louis was mine.

"So, fill me in on everyone. What they do, what they're like, that kind of thing," Leonie said as she curled her legs up under her.

I launched headfirst into a panic attack. According to custom (which was strictly enforced), Bombays didn't tell their spouses about the family until after they were married and before the first family reunion.

"Enough about my family—how about you? What's your family like?" *Ooh. Smooth.*

Leonie considered my question for a moment as she chewed the last of her bacon. "Well, I guess you'd say we're a bit unconventional."

Unconventional? I thought I had the market cornered on that.

"Oh, yeah," I remembered, "the family funeral home. You must have had an unusual childhood."

"I did. But for some morbid reason I liked it. We grew up with a strange sense of gallows humor. My dad's brother is also in the business. We have the largest funeral home in the state, back home."

I reached for the toast. "So, why did you want to break out on your own?" Was that too personal?

She shrugged. "I don't know. I guess I'm just kind of different from the rest of the family. They're more traditional. I never really fit in." She popped some more eggs into her mouth, and I got the impression that this line of conversation was over.

We spent the rest of breakfast talking about mundane things. The conversation wasn't memorable, but it had such an overwhelming sense of wonder to it.

While she was in the shower I thought

about everything. The way she made me feel—like I'd known her forever. The surge of emotion when we made love. How easily she fit in with my family. How much she loved my son. What started as a rush slowly became panic. By the time we were dressed I was beginning to sweat again. *Mental note—check the thermostat to see if it's set for hell.*

"I'm sorry, Dak," Leonie said with a frown. "I just got a call from the funeral home. Can you take me back to my car?"

I expelled a huge sigh of relief. For some reason I wanted her to go and stay at the same time. But I needed time to get my head together. I parked in front of my sister's house and walked Leonie to her car. She kissed me and winked as she jumped in and drove away.

I don't know how long I stood there on Gin's front lawn, staring after Leonie. I'm pretty sure it was a while, and that I would still be standing there had Louis not tackled me from behind. Gin waved me into the kitchen.

"Are you okay, mate?" Diego handed me a Diet Coke, and I nodded.

Gin was twittering nonstop about how wonderful Leonie was. I just sat there, mired in confusion. She didn't seem to notice.

"What is wrong with you?" Gin finally sat down next to me at the kitchen table.

"Huh? What do you mean?" I felt unstable. Kind of like I was homesick for . . . what?

"You haven't said a word." Gin frowned. "Oh, no! You're not breaking up with Leonie!"

"What?" I jumped. "No! I'm just . . . just a bit overwhelmed right now."

Diego nodded. "That makes sense. You got a new son, a big job from the Council, and a new girlfriend. That's a lot to deal with."

I looked at him. He was right. There was a lot on my plate. All of it was good individually, but together they twisted my insides mercilessly.

"At least the ED problem is over." Maybe that was one less thing to worry about.

"So why were you standing on my lawn for twenty-five minutes this morning, watching the road?" Gin grinned.

"You've got it bad, my friend," Diego said softly.

I looked at him. Diego understood probably more than I did. Last night felt like a triumph and a disaster at the same time. I had the feeling that a huge tidal wave was about to crush me at any second. And for a moment . . . just a moment . . . I thought it might be a good idea if it did.

Chapter Nineteen

"It's the end of the world as we know it, and I feel fine."

—R.E.M.

I know this is going to sound stupid, but I spent the rest of the day feeling really, really bad and really, really good at the same time. Gin and Diego kept me company in the backyard while we watched Louis and Romi play. No one spoke, which was good, because I had no idea what to say.

For the moment I was hung up on the fact that I had cried during sex. What did that mean? Shouldn't I just be grateful I was able to have an orgasm? But the idea of tears streaming down my face made me feel vulnerable and lost. Gin watched me with some interest. Every time she started to speak Diego shushed her. He's a good man.

Was I in love with Leonie? *Oh, my God.*

What was happening to me? Maybe I wasn't in love with her. Now, that thought hurt more.

I sat there for hours like that. Gin fed me lunch, then supper, then asked if I was spending the night. I looked at her as if she were speaking Swahili.

"Let's go home, Dad." Louis tugged on my sleeve. "*Survivor* is on, and we need to order pizza."

Oh, right. Our little ritual. Yes. We should do that. As we walked out the door I had another panic attack. I had a weekly ritual. With my son!

"You know what, Dad?" Louis said once we were back home. He looked at me very seriously, and I tried not to smile at the pizza sauce smeared on his chin.

"What's that?" I wiped his face, then pulled him a little closer.

"Well," he started, "I think we need to spend more time together." Louis raised his small hands to protest the words he thought would come—and if I weren't so shocked, I might have said something. "I mean, I know my arrival was inconvenient and that you have consulting work to do and all, but I can see that you and Leonie are getting serious, and I want to make sure you and I get to know each other too."

I sat there for a while, speechless. My son

had just told me he wanted to be with me. And while that should've made me feel great, he also said his arrival in my life was inconvenient and that he wanted to be as important as Leonie was. The sheer weight of this six-year-old's words crushed me like an aluminum can.

"Louis." I licked my lips to stall for time. "You are very important to me. You are never—and never will be—inconvenient. I'm sorry I made you feel like that." I was starting to get a little choked up.

"Leonie is important to me, but you are my son. Nothing in my life will ever be as important as you are. Do you understand that?" *Hell!* Did I understand what I was saying? All at once I felt ashamed of the way I'd been acting all day. I had practically ignored my own kid for a pity fest.

Louis scrutinized my face. My heart started to twist as I thought that he was trying to figure out whether what I said was bullshit or not. Before I could say anything else, Louis burrowed into my lap and sighed.

I held him for a long time. *Damn.* This kid had been through a lot. And here we started to get closer and I dumped him on Mom and Gin every day. No wonder he considered himself inconvenient.

After a while I realized he was asleep. As I

picked him up and carried him to bed I could feel his little heart beating. My son's heart had been broken when his mom died. Hell, he was probably scared to death when they brought him to me. I needed to prove to Louis that he came first and foremost. And this was probably the first time in my life that someone else did.

"You did *what*?" Paris chose to respond to my confession in a less sensitive way than I had hoped. All I could do was nod. I had told him about Leonie, hoping for advice. I wasn't ready to talk about Louis yet.

He sat back with a stunned look on his face. "Damn. Damn," was all he could say.

"I know. I don't know why I reacted like that." And I was feeling more than a little defensive.

"You've got it bad, man." Paris shook his head, but I noticed he didn't try to stifle a grin. *Bastard.*

"Can we just move on? What did you find out about the next guy on the list?" I wasn't just stalling. We needed to change the subject and get a move on. Our two weeks were almost up, and we'd knocked off only two of the five National Resources assassins.

Paris nodded, turning back to his laptop. "His name is Garth Stone, and he works at

Disney World. He's completely evil. He once hit a kid so his parents, in their grief, would sell their company to a conglomerate. I can't wait to get a crack at this asshole."

I swore under my breath, thinking about Louis. This bastard was going down as hard as possible.

"He plays Mickey Mouse at the Magic Kingdom six days a week," Paris continued.

I nodded, "Okay. We can do that. It's hard to see or hear in those costumes. We should be able to get the jump on him."

Paris looked at me as if I had sprouted two heads. "And just how do we kill Mickey Mouse in front of hundreds of kids?"

"I didn't say the plan was perfect. I just said the opportunity was better." He had a point. I didn't really want to scar the memories of a bunch of children as they watched Mickey Mouse spray blood all over them like a nightmarish lawn sprinkler.

"I've looked at a map of the Magic Kingdom. There's only one entrance and exit." Paris pointed at the map he placed in front of me. "And a *lot* of witnesses. We will also have to figure out disguises, because two thirty-something-year-old men in suits would stand out."

"Don't they have one of those gay-and-lesbian days there?" I asked. Paris shot me a look. "Okay, how about we go as Japanese tourists?"

Paris rolled his eyes, "Great. We're either homosexual lovers or we have to completely modify our physical features to look Asian." He tossed his hands up in the air. "I don't see how we can do it outside of finding out what his day off is."

I thought about that (mainly because it was better than thinking about my other problems). Figuring out his day off was too risky. There was no way to know when it would be and how we would find him. Great. We knew who he was and where he was. We just couldn't get to him. I examined the map. It was a long way from Toontown, where the soon-to-be-deceased Mickey signed autographs, and the exit. *Shit.*

My cell phone started to ring and I panicked for a moment, hoping it wasn't Leonie. I'd called her this morning (hey, I'm not a total cad!) and we made tentative plans to take Louis out for pizza tonight (and I know what you're thinking—pizza two nights in a row, but we'd order it with vegetables). But I was still scared of her and the way she made me feel.

Whew. Just Gin. I answered.

"Hey, Dak," Gin said breathlessly. "Now that you have a kid, and since next week is

spring break, I thought we could do something together with Liv. What do you think?"

I looked at Paris with a slow smile. "Sure,"
I answered. "I know exactly what we should
do."

Within an hour Paris had made all the
arrangements for a Bombay family trip to
Disney World. We had hotel accommodations
at the Contemporary for four days, Park
Hopper passes, flights, and everything. Gin,
Diego, Romi, Me, Louis, Paris, Liv, Todd, Alta,
and Woody would all go.

"So," Paris asked as he confirmed all the
reservations, "are we telling our sisters why
we're really going?"

I shook my head. "They'd be pissed and try
to stop us. Besides, Gin thinks I'm acting like
a real dad now. I'd hate to ruin that for her."

"Well, we leave in a few days. I think we
should knock out the Ohio zookeeper before
we go so we can at least report three of the
five kills to the Council."

"That's a good idea," I said.

"Let's go now—we can be there in about
eight hours."

I shook my head. "Can't do it tonight. I
promised Louis pizza."

Which is how Paris and I came to be in his
car, on the interstate to Tinker, Ohio, early

the next morning. Gin was thrilled with the spring break plans and happily agreed to take Louis for a few days. I had the strong suspicion that by the time I got back Gin and Liv would have cleaned the Disney Store in the mall out of clothing for all four kids.

I felt awful leaving Louis again—especially after our recent man-to-man. Before dropping him off I promised that this would be the last time I had to leave him for a while. And I intended to make good on that.

Tinker, Ohio, was twenty miles north of Columbus, a small town with its own zoo. And yes, we checked—they had bears. I patted the box with Missi's death-by-bear kit.

About ninety miles away from our destination my cell rang. I looked at Paris and answered it.

"Hey, Dela." I used my most charming tone.

"Cut the charisma, Dak. What's your status?"

Man. She wasn't buying it. *Okay, fine.* "Good. We've taken care of the dentist, the speaker, and, by this time tomorrow, the zookeeper. The next one is now a cast member at Disney World, so we're going there next week to take care of him. That just leaves the last one."

There was a sigh on the other end of the

GET UP TO
4 FREE BOOKS!

You can have the best romance delivered to your door for less than what you'd pay in a bookstore or online. Sign up for one of our book clubs today, and we'll send you **FREE* BOOKS** just for trying it out...**with no obligation to buy, ever!**

HISTORICAL ROMANCE BOOK CLUB

Travel from the Scottish Highlands to the American West, the decadent ballrooms of Regency England to Viking ships. Your shipments will include authors such as CONNIE MASON, CASSIE EDWARDS, LYNSAY SANDS, LEIGH GREENWOOD, and many, many more.

LOVE SPELL BOOK CLUB

Bring a little magic into your life with the romances of Love Spell—fun contemporaries, paranormals, time-travels, futuristics, and more. Your shipments will include authors such as KATIE MACALISTER, SUSAN GRANT, NINA BANGS, SANDRA HILL, and more.

As a book club member you also receive the following special benefits:

- **30% OFF all orders through our website & telecenter!**
  (Plus, you still get 1 book FREE for every 5 books you buy!)
- **Exclusive access to special discounts!**
- **Convenient home delivery and 10 days to return any books you don't want to keep.**

There is no minimum number of books to buy, and you may cancel membership at any time. See back to sign up!

*Please include $2.00 for shipping and handling.

YES! ☐

Sign me up for the **Historical Romance Book Club** and send my TWO FREE BOOKS! If I choose to stay in the club, I will pay only $8.50* each month, a savings of $5.48!

YES! ☐

Sign me up for the **Love Spell Book Club** and send my TWO FREE BOOKS! If I choose to stay in the club, I will pay only $8.50* each month, a savings of $5.48!

NAME: _____

ADDRESS: _____

_____

TELEPHONE: _____

E-MAIL: _____

☐ **I WANT TO PAY BY CREDIT CARD.**

☐ VISA ☐ MasterCard ☐ DISCOVER

ACCOUNT #: _____

EXPIRATION DATE: _____

SIGNATURE: _____

Send this card along with $2.00 shipping & handling for each club you wish to join, to:

**Romance Book Clubs
1 Mechanic Street
Norwalk, CT 06850-3431**

Or fax (must include credit card information!) to: 610.995.9274. You can also sign up online at www.dorchesterpub.com.

*Plus $2.00 for shipping. Offer open to residents of the U.S. and Canada only. Canadian residents please call 1.800.481.9191 for pricing information.

If under 18, a parent or guardian must sign. Terms, prices and conditions subject to change. Subscription subject to acceptance. Dorchester Publishing reserves the right to reject any order or cancel any subscription.

JOIN NOW!

phone. "All right. Just try to get it done before the end of next week. Undoubtedly the NR people have learned of the two deaths, so the rest will be on their guard."

"Roger that." I said. "Paris and I are working together, so we should be fine."

"I'll tell the Council," Dela replied. "Nice job with the zip line, by the way. I hated that bastard. Lou once ordered his tapes, and the whole Council spent a month listening to them." Then she clicked off.

"All's well," I said to Paris as I snapped my phone shut. And in my mind I really hoped that was true.

We checked into the Super 8 motel and changed into our disguises. Once again Paris arranged for the costumes, and once again I cursed him. Dressed in Wrangler jeans and cowboy boots, Ohio sweatshirts and baseball caps, we looked like any other average Joe. What I resented were the wigs. Why did they have to be mullets?

I slipped on my blond wig and stared at myself in the mirror. So this was what hell was like. Paris joined me in the mirror with his dark wig and a fake mustache. All I could think was, *Please don't let me die on this gig.*

The idea of dying on a job was one that

Bombays came to grips with at an early age. You never knew what could happen, really. We all carried cyanide capsules somewhere on our bodies. Gin had hers in a locket. Mine was in my ring. That's right, the one that got stuck in Leonie's hair. If I hadn't been able to get it up that night, I probably would've taken it.

The idea that you might die would be frightening if it weren't hammered into our subconscious at an early age. No one had ever died on a hit, thereby exposing the family. But just to be safe we never allowed ourselves to be fingerprinted.

I did *not* want to die with a mullet (there are just some things your reputation can't bounce back from). We'd have to be extra careful. Especially in case Dutch (our target) had found out about the deaths of his colleagues. Without a word we went out to the pickup truck Paris had rented under an assumed name and drove to the zoo.

This proved to be a good idea, because all we saw on the road were men in mullets and trucker caps, driving pickup trucks. Oddly enough we went unnoticed.

Paris circled the perimeter of the zoo twice, and I took notes of the entrances and exits. He pulled into the parking lot and we got out and, one at a time, bought tickets and entered. I was studying the zoo's map when Paris joined me.

"What do you think?" he asked quietly. His mustache was a little lopsided. I swallowed a smirk and responded by pointing out the bear enclosure on the map. We headed in that direction.

I've always liked bears. In this case it was three black bears in an enclosed area that gave the illusion it was completely open. The brochure said that they preferred to make it look like you could reach out and touch the animals. No cages were in evidence, but the bears were surrounded by a thirty-foot-wide-by-thirty-foot-deep cement moat.

Beary, the male, looked like he could handle the assignment. Missi had said black bears were unpredictable. The two females, Belle and Bebe, seemed docile. Beary stretched and looked at us, then rolled over and fell asleep.

"Hey," I asked a teenage kid wearing a staff shirt, "is Dutch around?"

The kid rolled his eyes. "He works the night shift tonight." Then the kid put earbuds in and turned up his iPod so loud I could hear some country singer wailing about Ford trucks.

Back in the room we checked our equipment and waited. We were glad Dutch had the night feeding shift. That way no one would be there to find his body until morning. Well, what was left of it, anyway.

Chapter Twenty

"And the number one threat to America is . . . bears!"
—Stephen Colbert, *The Colbert Report*

You know what's really stupid? Not locking the gates around a zoo at night. Granted, you probably don't have to worry about the animals escaping, but you do have to worry about someone like . . . well, like me.

Paris and I were crouched in some shrubbery near the bear enclosure. We'd been sitting there for some time, and my legs hurt.

"There he goes!" Paris whispered in my ear, and I squinted into the darkness to see that our prey was heading toward the bear pen. Surely it couldn't be this easy?

Without making any noise we slipped from our hiding place and followed Dutch into the darkness. I wasn't sure where we were going, but it looked like a cave. For a moment I hesitated, before I realized that this must be the entrance to the bear compound.

The faux cave had a heavy door with iron bars. Because Dutch had just gone in and thought he was alone, it was unlocked (what is it with Ohio?). We managed to squeeze through and close it without a sound, and waited until our eyes adjusted before proceeding.

I assumed—incorrectly, I might add—that there would be some sort of corridor . . . maybe a lab or something similar, before we entered the bears' lair. I was wrong. Within seconds I realized we were outside, and another second later I tripped over something large and furry.

A low grumble told me I wasn't in Kansas anymore. I didn't know which bear it was, and I didn't care. Scrambling to my feet, I somehow managed to jump free of his paw as it swiped out at me.

Shit! Shit! Shit!

"Dude," Paris asked quietly, "did you just trip over a bear?"

"Shh! He might hear you!" I hissed.

It was like I could *feel* Paris roll his eyes in the darkness. "Well, watch where you're going!"

Hysteria filled my voice. "I didn't think we were inside the bear thingie!"

"Who's there?" a deep voice boomed. "God-damned kids!"

Now what? We were trapped between our prey and a predator. The bear growled behind me. I saw a very large shadow moving toward us.

"Dutch!" Paris shouted, to my complete surprise. "Over here!"

"What the hell are you doing?" I whispered.

"Identifying our target." Paris shrugged, as if I were an idiot and we didn't have an angry bear behind us and an angry assassin in front of us.

"Yeah?" The voice was getting closer. "Who the fuck are you?"

Paris didn't answer. Instead he moved out of the bear's path and crouched down against the faux cave wall. I joined him, still not sure what his plan was.

Dutch loomed in front of us. Paris immediately flashed his LED light onto Dutch's arms, I guessed to search for the tattoo. The way the flesh on his arm twitched, it looked like Woody Woodpecker was laughing at us. Of course, that wasn't it—Dutch was just angry.

I grabbed the silver tube containing Missi's Bear Love Potion #9. I had to make the shot count, meaning it had to hit Dutch in order to attract the bear. I just wanted to get the job done.

Dutch decided to charge us. The silver tube was slippery in my fingers, but I managed to find the button and push it. There was a sharp cry and I felt some satisfaction. We'd have only a few seconds before our vic realized he'd just been doused to smell like a cross between an appetizer and an attractive bear whore.

I could feel the beast moving now. Its four feet slapping against the ground rumbled like thunder (thunder with sharp claws and teeth). Paris ran off as fast as the bear closed in on us.

Wait a minute. Why was the bear closing in on us? Dutch was about fifty feet away in the other direction. I could smell the barbecue sauce. So why wasn't Beary (I decided it was the male—for my own ego's sake) heading for him?

In the darkness I saw the four-legged eating machine racing after Paris. The smell of tangy ribs seemed to be fading. Why was that? I looked at Dutch, who suddenly seemed to appear closer than he really was. Paris was screaming now, running in a zigzag formation across the compound.

I watched in confusion, forgetting about Dutch. That is, until he punched me in the side of the head. As I fell to the ground, I realized what had happened. I hadn't hit Dutch with the spray. I hit Paris. Now he was in danger of becoming Beary's midnight snack/new girlfriend, and I was getting my ass kicked by another assassin. Some days it just doesn't pay to get out of bed, drive to Ohio, and put on a mullet wig.

Chapter Twenty-one

O-Ren Ishii: "You didn't think it was gonna be that easy, did you?"
The Bride: "You know, for a second there, yeah, I kinda did."

—*Kill Bill: Volume One*

Paris ran by, screaming again. Good thing for him he was going pretty fast. Beary would eventually catch up, though. And I had to do something about it before he did.

Unfortunately Dutch wasn't in a Good Samaritan kind of mood. He must have figured out we weren't a couple of teenagers breaking in for fun. Mainly I gathered this from what he said as he hauled me to my feet.

"Who sent you?"

If I were inclined to do so, I would've answered him. But that was impossible, because he punctuated each question with a punch to my gut. I responded by kicking his knee backward until I heard it crunch.

Dutch screamed and dropped to the ground—his left leg bent like an inverted V, which made his mouth turn into the letter O. He still had hold of my collar, so I went down with him.

"Will you hurry up and help me?" Paris shrieked as he ran by again. I hoped he'd change his running pattern soon, or Beary would figure it out and ambush him. Bears are smart that way.

I brought both arms up in front of me, over the shoulder and down, breaking Dutch's hold. After scrambling a safe distance away I fumbled for Missi's bear tube. Finding it, I managed to load it and squeeze off another shot, hitting Dutch with a satisfying *plink*.

Dutch, my vic, was so freaked out about his leg being bent backward, he didn't even notice. But I did see Belle's and Bebe's noses go up in the air. There was no time to waste waiting to see if Dutch would actually be eaten by the bear, so I shot him, using Missi's disintegrating bullets. He looked up at me in surprise before falling over dead.

"Aaaaaaaaaaaaaaaaah!" Paris shrieked as he ran by me again. This time, however, Beary noticed the smell coming from Dutch. He slowed down just enough to sniff in that direction.

"Hey!" I shouted. "Make another loop, then head straight for the cave door!" I turned and ran to the hidden cave door, swinging it open and holding it in place.

My barbecue-scented cousin ran through, and I managed to close the door on Beary's head. Paris helped me hold it until we locked it. Then, without looking back, we ran until we made it to the car.

"Dammit!" Paris shouted from the shower for what must've been the fifteenth time. "It's not coming off!"

I didn't respond. This was beyond my saying anything. I just folded his shirt up into a hotel towel and shoved it into a duffel. I did make a mental note to tell Missi that the bear juice went straight through clothing and stayed on the skin for hours. The whole trip back was like riding with a giant McRib sandwich. I think Paris was a little offended when I pulled up to a barbecue-pork restaurant for takeout on the way back.

"That was messy," Paris grumbled.

I nodded. "I didn't leave anything behind, and they're likely to miss the bullet wound if he was mauled and eaten."

But in spite of our success, I didn't feel good about the hit. It was too sloppy. Chances were we'd hear about it from the Council.

It took several hours to get home, and after picking up Louis and putting him to bed, I concentrated more on my injuries. Cleaning up at the hotel before leaving helped somewhat, but I still felt bruised all over.

Sure enough, there were telltale marks on my abdomen where Dutch had hit me repeatedly. No swimming at Disney World. It would be too noticeable, and I didn't know how to explain it to Louis. *Well, Daddy was trying to kill this guy, but he kept punching me in the stomach.* Somehow that line of conversation didn't seem helpful.

The next morning, after delivering the little guy to school, I met up with Leonie for lunch. She looked tired. I guess you didn't really get much sleep as a mortician. It wouldn't necessarily be a nine-to-five job.

"I was wondering when I'd hear from you again." She smiled wryly.

"Sorry." I ran my right hand through my hair. "Had to go out of town on business. But I'm back now. How are things at Crummy's?"

Leonie looked at me curiously for a moment, and I found myself wondering what she really thought of me. Her light blue eyes cut me to the quick.

"I'm not mocking you, by the way. But it is hard to say the name of your business without sounding sarcastic," I managed.

She arched her right eyebrow, and her

scowl faded into a smile. "Oh. Yeah. Right." Leonie waved her hand, and I found myself wanting to suck on those long, slender fingers. "There's just a lot going on—period. It's nothing, really."

As she talked about her most recent funeral, I discovered that I was completely wrapped around every word that came from that lovely mouth. I did have it bad. But I didn't care. She was everything I wanted . . . everything I needed. And I was an idiot to let her out of my sight for one minute. Of course, that would mean hanging out at the funeral home, and I didn't really want to see what went on downstairs, if you catch my drift.

"So what about you?" Leonie lifted the glass of wine to her lips, and I swooned.

"Oh, not much. Consulting stuff here and there. Next week is spring break, so my whole family is going to Disney World."

Leonie laughed. "I wish I could go with you. It would be much better than consoling the bereaved and embalming the deceased."

"Do you actually do that? The embalming, I mean?" I guess it never occurred to me that my beloved (who, by the way, didn't know she was my beloved yet) could drain and refill a dead body. Of course, I could drain one too—using bullets as a colander.

She nodded. "It's not so bad. I guess I've

been around it all my life, so I'm kind of used to it." She pointed to my ribs with her fork. "You gonna eat that?"

Suddenly my taste for barbecued flesh had run its course. I shook my head and she scooped the rack of ribs off my plate.

Oh, well, grossed out or not, I loved Leonie Doubtfire. And after dropping her back off at Crummy's with a lingering, lusty kiss, I made up my mind to tell her that the minute I got back from killing Mickey. I mean, when I got back from the Bombay Family Magical Gathering at Disney World.

Chapter Twenty-two

"You are traveling through another dimension, a dimension not only of sight and sound but of mind. A journey into a wondrous land of imagination. Next stop, the Twilight Zone."

—Rod Serling, *The Twilight Zone*

Sure enough, Gin and Liv went wild buying Disney clothes for all four kids. Mom was a little miffed that we were going—apparently she'd been planning to take Romi and Louis in the fall.

There was something about Disney World that brought out the kid in me. I'd never been, but every moment from the bus ride to the hotel to the minute we set foot in the Magic Kingdom, I felt like a five-year-old again. Diego, Todd, and Paris seemed to watch me, Gin and Liv with amusement as we "oohed" and "ahhed" over everything from the rides to the gardens to the Mickey Mouse ear hats (mine said, *Dakota*.)

The first day we just kind of shuffled from place to place, checking everything out. And

I loved it all. It was as if this magical place had been made specially, just for me. I couldn't get enough of the sights, smells, and sounds.

Mostly I couldn't get enough of watching Louis enjoying himself. Except for a few exceptionally brilliant comments like, "They must use dry ice to get that smoke," and, "Did you realize there are no straight lines on Mickey's house? The contractors must've had it rough," he seemed like any other kid. I decided that as soon as this job was over and school was out, the two of us would take a trip somewhere. Just me and my son.

About midday, I started to notice something. At first Louis wanted to go on the rides with his cousins. But on the Peter Pan ride he asked if he could ride with me. I scooped him up and climbed into the boat that carried us through Neverland. Every ride after that Louis wanted to sit with me.

"Hey, Dad," Louis said quietly. "I want to be just like you someday."

"What do you mean?" I asked before thinking about it.

He took a deep breath, like he was going to say something you'd expect from a thirty-year-old, not a kid. "I mean that someday I want to take my son to Disney World and ride the rides with him, just like you."

I looked at him for a moment. He had a funny way of completely surprising me. "Well, kiddo, I hope I can be right there with you both."

He smiled, and I realized that my answer seemed to be enough—even if I didn't know what the hell the question was.

We spent the second day at the Animal Kingdom, riding rides, seeing parades, and touring the animal treks. Louis seemed to know more about the wildlife than the cast members who minded the Komodo dragon, naked mole rats, and fruit bats.

I bought him a stuffed bat at the gift shop, and Louis grinned his little gap-toothed grin.

"Thanks, Dad. You're awesome."

I felt a little spring in my step. Yep, I was about fifty pounds lighter. Funny how something so simple made me feel so great.

"Hey, Louis?" I asked.

"What?" answered my perfect son.

I gazed into his intelligent little face before answering, "Chicken butt."

Louis tilted his head to one side, and for a moment I thought he wouldn't get it. There wasn't any logic, rhyme, or reason to it. It was just funny to say that when someone said, "What?" At least, it had been when I was a kid.

Louis burst into a fit of giggles, and I realized that no matter how supersmart he was, we could both laugh about the business end of a chicken. I was having a great time.

We were just about to get on the Kali River Rapids when an overwhelming sense of familiarity hit me. There was something about the man running the ride that screamed in my head. But he didn't look like anyone I knew. Tall, muscular, and rugged-looking, the blond man looked exactly like the actor Daniel Craig. That was odd. Why would Daniel Craig be working there? In fact, I was feeling a little threatened by his attractiveness. I'd never had the "all-man" look. I was more the boyish rogue.

"Coney?" Gin gasped, and the rest of us turned to look at him.

He smiled. "I guess my own family doesn't recognize me." He finished shoving our backpacks into the middle tube so they wouldn't get wet.

My jaw dropped open as Paris said, "Hey, man! You look so different! How could we recognize you?"

Coney laughed and said, "Tell you what: I'll meet you at Wolfgang Puck's in Downtown Disney for dinner at eight." We barely had time to nod in agreement as he shoved our raft away. We were soaked by the very first wave, but all of us still had that look of shock on our faces. I got water in my mouth; it was still open.

When we got off the ride he was gone. Soaked to the skin, all ten of us kind of waddled back to the bus to the hotel. We managed to clean up and head out to Downtown Disney while Gin filled Diego and Todd in on our strangest relative.

"He has a Ph.D. in philosophy from an Ivy League school. And he's a carny," Liv explained.

I watched as Diego's eyebrows arched in surprise. It was true. In fact, the last time I saw Coney Island Bombay was at the family reunion last fall. His head was shaved bald, he had a beard, and he was covered in tattoos. In spite of the way he looked, Coney was a good guy. The carny lifestyle seemed to suit him. He traveled the country in a tricked-out RV, wealthy housewives fell all over him to satisfy their carny sex fantasies, and he wintered in Florida. In between all that, he read things by Jean-Paul Sartre, Nietzsche, and John Stuart Mill . . . just for fun.

In fact, he always reminded me of Doc Savage; supersmart, muscular frame, laid-back philosophical attitude, all that. Well, except for the assassin part. Doc always rehabilitated the criminals he caught. He wasn't big on the death penalty.

Upon entering Wolfgang Puck's, we found him immediately, sitting at a table in a blue silk shirt and tan linen slacks that made him look like he was about to order a martini shaken, not stirred. After we made introductions and were seated, Paris blurted out the big question.

"Dude! You look so different! What happened?"

Coney leaned back, taking a very manly drink from his expensive scotch, and smiled. "I'm kind of going through a new phase."

The waitress arrived with coloring books and crayons and took our drink orders.

"But the tattoos?" Liv asked.

"They were never real. Missi developed a special semipermanent ink that, with a certain solvent, could be erased from the skin completely. I'm kind of done with them. Taking a philosophical sabbatical here."

"At Disney World?" I asked, feeling a little like an idiot.

Coney smiled, and I thought what a handsome, self-assured man he was.

"It's what I know. I like it. I do this every now and then." He looked at the kids, then me. "So, you've changed a bit too."

I nodded. "Yeah. It was a surprise to me as well. But Louis is awesome." I realized I was grinning like an idiot. I was proud of him.

We talked for a long time, through dinner, dessert, and more drinks. Looking at the end of the table I could see that the kids were getting pretty tired. Diego and Todd noticed it too, because they volunteered to take them back to the hotel so that all of us cousins could hang out. Gin and Liv kissed their husbands and waved as they left.

"We should get out of here," Coney said, throwing a couple of crisp hundred dollar bills on the table. "How about a nightcap?"

Gin, Liv, Paris, Coney, and I headed across the bridge to Pleasure Island. We settled at a table in one of the clubs and continued talking. Then a bunch of songs from the eighties came on, and before we could respond Gin and Liv ran squealing to the dance floor.

"So, what brings you here?" Coney asked.

Paris popped another Mickey Mouse–shaped pretzel into his mouth. "A job. From the Council."

We filled Coney in on everything. When we finished he leaned back in his chair and had another drink of his scotch.

"His name is Garth Stone, eh? Haven't met him yet. How are you going to approach it?"

Paris and I looked at each other and shrugged. "We kind of thought we were lucky just to get this far," Paris answered.

Coney looked toward the dance floor, where

Gin and Liv were dancing. I followed his line of vision and was horrified to discover that all the moves I thought were cool in the eighties actually must have made me look like a spastic heron with rickets. "Karma Chameleon" was playing, and I realized that at my fiftieth high school reunion, a bunch of ugly old people would be dancing to it and saying how timeless the music of our generation was. I shuddered.

"You said they don't know about the job?" Coney nodded toward our sisters.

I shook my head. "Paris and I would be smoked if they knew. They think we're here to bond with the kids."

Actually, Paris and I had toyed with the idea of getting Gin and Liv involved. But no matter how we looked at it, it just seemed to be a really horrible idea.

"Here's what I know," Coney said to us once the waitress laid down a new round of alcohol. "You'll never find him on his day off. The younger kids—interns—they run around the parks on their days off. I speak from some level of experience when I say that a thirty- or forty-something assassin won't do that. And since this zookeeper knew you were coming, Garth will be on the lookout. I'd suggest you deal with the costume."

"The costume? What do you mean?" Paris

asked, sipping his Manhattan. I guess I never really noticed before that he drank as if he were Angie Dickinson. Then I remembered he had a Pink Cadillac at dinner and decided I needed to talk to him about that later.

"I'd rig his costume to kill him," Coney suggested. "It's the only way I can think of to get the job done without doing it directly."

"How would you do it?" I asked.

Coney rubbed his chin. "I'd undo the lining of the neck on the headpiece and put about three wraps of det cord around the inside. Install the detonator and attach the wireless device. Ensure that it's turned on, and then close it back up. Use your cell phone to trigger the explosion. If you do it right everything will happen inside the costume, and with a muffled pop he'll just fall over."

We looked at him, blinking like those toads that need their eyes to swallow.

"You've thought about doing this before, haven't you?" I asked.

Coney smiled. "Oh, only about a thousand times. Those costume guys can be real dicks to us ride jockeys."

Gin and Liv joined us, and we spent another couple of hours laughing about the family. It was a definite source of amusement.

The night ended with us getting a group photo of our heads superimposed on *Star*

Wars characters. Paris was Luke Skywalker, Coney was Han Solo, and I had to be Chewbacca. *Huh.* Maybe it was a metaphor for the way things were going.

After this there was only one assassin left to take out. The trip made me realize how important Leonie and family were to me. I was pretty confident the Council would give us a lot of time off. Five hits in less than one month was the stuff of legend to the Bombays. Then I could sort everything out. Yes, things were definitely looking up.

Chapter Twenty-three

Male Muppet: "Mah nah mah nah."
Female Muppets: "Doo doo, de doo doo!"
Male Muppet: "Mah nah mah nah."
Female Muppets: "Doo doo doo doo!"
Male muppet: "Mah nah mah nah."
Female Muppets: "Doo doo, de doo doo, de doo doo, de doo doo doo de doo doo doo doo doo!"

—*Sesame Street*

Of course, things looked different in the cold light of morning than they had the night before. At least, this was what Paris and I thought as we stood in front of the costume department in the Magic Kingdom.

How did we find it? It wasn't easy. There were no maps to show the secret employee hideouts. And the slight hangover from the night before didn't really put Paris and me in the best mood. Eventually Paris managed to find a bribable cast member. The one-hundred-dollar bill and the elaborate story he gave Snow White about how he planned to propose to his girlfriend by surprising her in costume helped.

The entrance to the costume warehouse was cleverly disguised as a wall and we weren't exactly sure where to find the door. We'd convinced the family to stop for a snack while Paris and I surveilled the place. After an eternity (do you know it is nearly impossible to eat a batch of french fries very, very slowly? I was so hungry I practically ate my own fingers in the process), the wall opened and Buzz Lightyear popped out. Within seconds he was mobbed by kids, and we had our answer.

Because we had no way of getting det cord, Coney volunteered to set us up. When we got back to our rooms that night, a comatose Louis slung over my shoulder, we found a Disney bag filled with everything we needed.

I nudged Louis awake, against his will, and handed him over to Todd with the lie that he wanted to sleep with their son, Woody. Whether they bought it or not, Liv and her husband accepted my boy wordlessly and tucked the two kids in together.

Paris and I waited until we heard everyone in the adjoining rooms go to bed before slipping into our *Mission Impossible* gear. We'd gotten too far to have Gin and Liv bust us just to borrow aspirin.

As we sat there silently in the darkness feeling like idiots, my mind started to wander. Before this trip I'd never been to Disney World. Sure, I knew it was hailed as the happiest place on earth, but when the plane landed in Orlando, I had thought it would be just like any other theme park.

I was wrong—and I don't admit that very often. Something about the place from the minute we checked into our hotel told me to relax, have fun, that time didn't matter here. The kids whooped and hollered, and we adults all seemed to have goofy grins on our faces. I started to think that for once, maybe the Bombay family could be like any other family. Maybe we could pretend we were normal people. What would that be like?

Of course, then I remembered that we weren't like any other family on vacation at Disney World. We came here with a purpose other than meeting Mickey Mouse. We came here to kill him.

There were two ways to handle the situation. The Magic Kingdom was technically shut down for the night, but we knew there was a whole crew of employees who worked through the night to scrape gum off the ground, weed the flowers, and basically make it look like there weren't forty thousand people there the day before. We could either disguise ourselves as maintenance people or sneak in. I didn't want to work that hard—so we donned our ski masks and black clothes for the job.

Breaking into the Magic Kingdom isn't as easy as you might think. But I'd hardly be professionally responsible if I divulged their secrets, so suffice it to say that Paris and I made it into the park and to the warehouse undetected.

I truly admire the way Disney World operates. Paris and I had planned on being there for several hours. That's how it usually works. We'd have to find the costume, confirm if and when Garth would be wearing it, and dodge staff.

That was why it was such a surprise to find a clipboard hanging from Mickey Mouse's suit listing Garth as the first one to wear it the next day. The clipboard confirmed he would be in Toontown. *Damn.* Disney should branch out into the assassination business. They could lure bad guys to the park and take them out and clean up afterward so no one would ever know. Maybe I should talk to Grandma about that—bring them on as a subcontractor.

"That was way too easy," Paris said quietly once we made it back to our room. He pulled off his stealth clothes and climbed into pajamas. I did a cartoon double take. Were those sock monkeys on his jammies? How did I not notice this before? My amusement at all things Paris was starting to turn into concern.

"But maybe the Fates are cutting us some slack after the bear job," he added as he slid under the covers.

I ran my hands through my hair. "I hope so. I don't want to blow up the wrong guy tomorrow."

I looked in the mirror with curiosity. My reflection told me my cool was slipping away. My hair looked messy, not styled, and my eyes looked tired, not full of fun. This job was getting to me. And I couldn't wait for it to be over.

Paris rolled over in his bed. "We won't. It's all set. Then there's just one more." His breathing began to slow, and I realized he was asleep.

I also realized that I was bone-tired. Maybe I was getting too old for this shit. *No*, I told myself, *it's just having to kill so many people in so short a time. No one's ever had to do that before in the family.*

I'd never been the sort of guy who looked for answers in his life. To me, killing people was just something I was good at. I had no qualms about the assholes I took out. It helped that I knew they were inherently bad people. I slept okay at night.

Gin had had a run-in with her conscience when she hooked up with Diego. Taking down your bodyguard boyfriend's client will do that to you. Liv got off on taking out neo-conservatives. Paris didn't seem bothered.

Coney popped into my mind, and I thought that maybe the reason he was so drawn to philosophy was to find a way to make sense of it all. I never had much use for philosophy, unless it helped me score with some chick.

I rolled over and stared at the wall. This line of thought was stupid. Garth, Munch, Dutch, and Lowe were assassins. They didn't have the family tradition we had, and, as I'd learned with each of them, they were stone-cold killers, taking out innocent people. Hell, Garth had taken out a kid for profit! I hung on to that thought for a moment. They were killers.

But so was I. *Christ*, I thought, *I'm getting nowhere with this. Stop analyzing! Just do the job and get the hell out of Orlando.* One more job and our competition would be wiped out.

I thought about Coney and his pursuit of answers. Suddenly my shallowness didn't seem so stupid. Life in the Bombay family was definitely better if you didn't try to face all your demons—even if he was a cute rodent wearing red pants and a killer smile.

Chapter Twenty-four

"It happens sometimes. People just explode. Natural causes."

—Agent Rogersz, *Repo Man*

Toontown was crowded, which was good. It's easy to get lost in a crowd. Unfortunately there would be a lot of witnesses too, but that couldn't be helped.

The whole family was waiting in line to see Mickey Mouse and Chip and Dale. And even though I should've kept my mind on the job, I had to wonder if anyone knew who the hell Chip and Dale were. I mean, come on! I'm thirty-seven and I barely remember their cartoons as a kid.

Louis, Romi, Alta, and Woody were waiting to see the damned chipmunks. Paris and I made sure they'd already met Mickey earlier, so they wouldn't feel robbed of that special experience when he imploded. If we'd rigged the shape charges right there'd be a noise, and Mickey would collapse to the floor with no mess. We'd hustle the kids out so they didn't see the Garth soup inside the costume.

As we stepped up for the kids to meet the chipmunks, I nodded slightly at Paris. He, in turn, took out his cell phone and aimed it at the kids as if he were going to take a picture. Only he and I knew that we were actually triggering the mechanism that would blow up a beloved Disney character/National Resources assassin.

Paris waited until Mickey was alone and pressed the button.

There was a muffled explosive sound, kind of like *ffffoooom*, and the Mickey Mouse head shot into the air. Mickey's body fell to the floor backward, fortunately hiding what was left of Garth's head.

Some people noticed the noise; others didn't seem to register it. The Mickey head (sans the ears—apparently they were blown off) came down in front of Chip and Dale, who, because of difficulties seeing through their costumes, thought some kid had thrown them a large beach ball. Thus, to my amazement and everyone else's horror, they started tossing the battered head back and forth.

The cast member who was handling Mickey screamed, and suddenly everything came back to the present. Paris and I faked shock as we dragged our family out of the barn and outside. Three of the kids looked stunned. Louis, however, was frowning. I didn't have time to worry about it as Paris and I hustled everyone onto the Lilly Belle train for our getaway.

The train seemed like a good idea when we had planned it. It runs the perimeter of the park to the front entrance. No fighting through crowds, no walking. Easy, right? We'd be out of Toontown before security arrived.

Do you know how slow that damned train is? I felt like an idiot, trying to get away from the scene of the crime on a vehicle that goes *toot! toot!* at four miles per hour.

Looking at everyone in the group, I thought that the kids managed relatively unscathed. Diego told them that Mickey wasn't feeling well, so he fainted but was okay. Todd backed this up with a funny story about something including a rhinoceros and a Pomeranian. Romi and Alta bought it. Woody wisely kept his mouth shut, and Louis was staring at me.

Actually, so were Gin and Liv. Well, they weren't exactly staring so much as trying to kill us with a look. I wondered if you could really do that. It would be so much more effective. I'd have to talk to Missi.

After what seemed like ten hours we made

it to the entrance and hopped on the monorail to the hotel. Gin and Liv had their arms crossed over their chests and were still glaring at Paris and me. I was pretty sure they'd figured out what happened.

We hadn't discussed the job with them. In fact, they knew we'd been working on a Council assignment but never asked about it. From the looks on their faces, our sisters knew now.

Todd and Diego seemed to know something was up, because they volunteered to take the kids to the pool. Liv and Gin followed us to our room, not saying a word and definitely not invited. Paris and I tolerated it because we didn't know what else to do.

"You killed Mickey Mouse?" Gin hissed before the door had fully closed.

"I don't believe this!" Liv threw her hands up in the air. "That's why we're on this trip, isn't it?"

"How could you drag your family into this?" Gin was on a tear.

"Now, hold on," Paris said, his hands up and forming a barrier between him and his angry sister. "This is just a job. And it's not like the Bombays don't know that."

I nodded. "You used to do this for a living, remember? The rest of us didn't get retirement."

And that was when Gin slapped me across the face. At least it wasn't a right cross.

"You could've told us! We could've taken the kids somewhere else!" Liv shouted.

"No, we needed them to be there," Paris said simply.

Oh, shit. Here it comes.

"You used the kids as your cover!" Gin said through her teeth. "How could you do that to them?"

Liv had a dangerous look in her eyes, and for once I thought my earth-mother cousin was going to kill us.

"Okay," I conceded, "it was wrong. We know that. But the Council ordered us to get the job done. We had no choice."

Gin shook her head. "I don't buy it. You could have found another way."

"I can't believe you'd drag Louis into this!" Liv said.

"Louis has to begin his training too, like your kids," Paris said slowly. "It's not like we have an option to exclude them."

Gin crossed her arms over her chest again. I was a little nervous she might have a shoulder holster on. "What about Todd and Diego? You didn't need to drag them into it."

I sat down on the edge of the bed. I had nothing. While I was happy to have four of the five hits done, there was something in what she said that made me feel guilty.

"Well, it's over now," Paris said with a sigh.

"Maybe you should tell us exactly what *it* is." Liv folded her arms too.

So we told them everything. How five people ranging from Gin's oral surgeon to Mickey Mouse were dangerous assassins who killed innocent people, including children. We might have played up the danger a bit by saying they were coming after the Bombays. But that could've been true. Gin had known about Munch by being there. What she didn't know was that we had to take out a whole company.

Liv and Gin listened carefully, still glowering—which, by the way, was not a good look for them. I toyed with telling them that at their age they couldn't afford new wrinkles, but a strong sense of self-preservation told me this wasn't the time.

No one spoke for a few moments, which, I must admit, made me a little nervous. If I hadn't had a son depending on me, I do believe Gin and Liv would've killed us on the spot.

"Well," Gin said grudgingly, "I still don't think you had to handle the last one this way."

Liv reacted differently. "You were chased by a hungry bear?" She seemed to struggle not to burst out laughing.

"It wasn't my fault!" Paris whined. "Dak had lousy aim."

"Yeah, but you screamed like Romi on Space Mountain." I had to smile, remembering that.

"Go to hell," Paris said halfheartedly.

"I'm sure we'll all be there someday." Gin scowled. "I do wish I could've seen what happened at the zoo. It would've made for great blackmail material. I'd love to hold that over you for the rest of your life."

We spent the last night at Disney World quietly: dinner at the restaurant on top of the Contemporary followed by one last fireworks show over the Magic Kingdom. Louis was very quiet, and I wondered if he was just exhausted or worried about the man in the Mickey Mouse suit.

First thing in the morning we all packed up and headed to the airport. It took a long time to get through security, and I wondered why I didn't think of chartering our private jet. By the end of the day we were back in the Midwest.

"All set, champ?" I sat on Louis's bed that night.

He nodded solemnly. "Thanks for the trip, Dad. I really liked it. Well, except for when Mickey Mouse's head blew off. But I loved the rest of it."

I wasn't sure what to say. Obviously my kid was smart enough to know that an explosion had occurred. I kissed him on the forehead and tucked him in.

"So, why did you do it?" he asked casually.

"Do what?" My palms started to sweat.

"Kill Mickey Mouse," Louis said. "I saw Paris use his cell phone to do it." His big eyes were hard on mine, and I was pretty sure my spleen had burst. How the hell did he figure it out? For once I thought maybe it wasn't so great to have a smart kid.

"You're not answering me." Louis frowned.

So I did what millions of parents have done over thousands of years: I bluffed. "What makes you think we killed Mickey Mouse?"

My son rolled his eyes at me (okay, so my poker face had abandoned me). "It wasn't Mickey Mouse—just a man in a suit. And it was pretty obvious. Have you been an assassin for very long?"

It felt as if Louis's words were pummeling me. I couldn't lie to the kid—at least, not now. I had no experience in handling this. My dad learning curve was pretty short.

"All right." I sat up a little straighter. "It's time you knew the truth about the Bombay family."

Two hours and an entire stuffed-crust cheese pizza later, Louis knew his family history. He took it well, considering he just found out he'd be doing contract kills for the rest of his life.

"That explains why everyone is so rich and no one works." Louis chewed his pizza thoughtfully. "It's bad guys, right?"

"Well, that's the story, for the most part," I responded. "They don't really give us a dossier on each hit. We assume the Council knows what it's doing."

"And I have to start my training?" Louis looked a little perplexed.

"Soon." I stole a look at the clock. "But right now you have to get some sleep. It's very late. Oh, and Louis?" I hesitated. "We don't talk about this outside the Bombay family."

My kid nodded, then used his pajama sleeve as a napkin and curled up to sleep.

I hit the bottle of scotch in the kitchen. I felt like I'd just unleashed hell on the world. That was ridiculous. Louis would be a perfect killer. He'd research everything and be completely careful.

It surprised me how well he took the news. Maybe the fact that he knew his cousins were dealing with this helped. He was only six. There was plenty of time to cope with the ramifications. I didn't think I had to worry about seeing any Junie B. Jones books called *I Was a First-grade Assassin*.

Eventually I went to sleep, and I dreamed of exploding Disney characters.

Chapter Twenty-five

"The extreme always seems to make an impression."

—J.D., *Heathers*

After dropping my soon-to-be-lethal son at school, I called Leonie and set up a date for that night. Mom told me the minute we got back that she was babysitting—no matter what. I figured Louis would have a million questions about family and that Mom was the perfect person to answer them.

Something had been bothering me for a while, so that night, as we settled on my couch, I asked Leonie the big question.

"What's your favorite color?"

Leonie choked on her beer. "What? Why?"

"Because I'm afraid I'm moving too fast, and I don't know you as well as I should."

She arched her eyebrows in what I took to be amusement.

"I want to get to know you intellectually . . .

in addition to physically." That wasn't hard. So why was I nervous? It seemed like a perfectly normal question. Maybe it was too personal? *Listen to me! I'm in love with this woman and I'm too scared to ask her favorite color. Maybe I should be drinking Pink Cadillacs.*

"What?" I was suddenly aware that she was talking to me.

"You asked what my favorite color is," she said patiently, "and it's cerulean."

"Jesus," I said, taking a drink of beer, "what would Freud say about that?"

Leonie laughed. "He'd say that sometimes cerulean is just cerulean."

"Blue. Your favorite color is blue. Why can't you just say blue?" I have to admit it irritated me that she had to pick a color so obscure that Crayola didn't use it. And these are the folks who came up with periwinkle.

"Cerulean, like the color of your eyes when I make love to you."

I tried not to let the fact that my body was already getting hard distract me.

"Fine. I concede that your favorite color is a ten-dollar word for blue."

Leonie grinned. "And yours? Didn't you tell me once that you liked blue?"

I stuck out my chin defiantly. "No. I have grown as a person over the years. My multitude of experiences have enlightened and shaped me into a mature adult." I paused dramatically. "I like red now."

Leonie laughed again. You know how there's a frequency of sound that only dogs can hear? Well, there was something in that laugh that I swear only my dick could hear.

"Have I answered the question to your satisfaction?" She arched her right eyebrow.

"You have won the day this time, evildoer," My loins were begging me to end this stupid line of questioning. "But I'll be back, and when I am, you will submit to my interrogation."

"Do your worst," she challenged, "but for now I will claim my prize." Leonie pulled me toward the bedroom. As she pushed me onto the bed I thought that at this rate, getting to know her intellectually was going to take a long, long time.

Cerulean! I mean, *really!*

Two hours later we found ourselves sitting in the kitchen (me in my boxers and Leonie in my shirt—and she looked better than me in it) eating whatever was in my fridge.

"Mmmmmmm." Leonie licked some honey off her fingers. "This is so good I could go into brain lock."

I paused from eating cottage cheese out of the container with a spoon. *What?*

"Brain lock? Is that dangerous?"

She shrugged. "When iguanas have too much information to process, they go into a kind of brain lock where they shut down to figure out how to deal with it."

"You can't be serious."

"It's true." She grinned. "I once had an iguana."

"An iguana, eh?" I asked. "You were into lizards?"

"Hey!" Leonie said, a little defensively. "Cecil was great. I don't think they're as affectionate as dogs, but he liked to climb on me for the body warmth."

"I guess I have something in common with Cecil then." I winked at her. "Whatever happened to him?"

"It's a long story," she said, biting her lip, and I got the feeling she didn't want to tell me.

"It looks like we have time. Besides, we are trying to learn more about each other, right?"

"A friend of Mom's gave him to me. He had outgrown his cage and at six feet long was beginning to threaten their cats. I only had him for a little while. He died three months later."

"What happened?" I couldn't believe I was in love with an iguana lady.

"His owners had been feeding him cat food for two years. That's okay for a baby, but once he was six months old he needed fruits and vegetables. His organs calcified."

"Did you know something was wrong?"

"His toes would tap, like he had Parkinson's. I took him to the zoo, and they sent me to a vet. He sent me home after drawing blood and told me to give him a warm bath. I left him in the tub for a minute, and when I came back he was lying on the bottom, underwater."

"He drowned?"

"No, iguanas are good swimmers. He just died. Anyway, are you sure you want to hear more?"

"Absolutely."

She gave me a stern look. "You're not mocking me, are you?"

"Never." I placed my hand over my heart. "Go on."

Leonie took a deep breath and continued. "I took him out of the tub and put him on the floor. He opened his mouth and gasped. So I did what any other iguanatarian would do."

"Iguanatarian?" Could she just make up words like that?

"I, um, gave him mouth-to-mouth and chest massage."

I'd bet Leonie had gotten used to the eruption of hysterical laughter over the years. For some reason, she'd never been smart enough not to tell the story in the first place.

I finished laughing and wiped my eyes. "I'm sorry. Did you really try to resuscitate him?"

Leonie nodded, and I had the feeling she didn't want to take the story any further. Unfortunately for her, I'm a cruel bastard.

"Did it work?" I pressed.

"No. Adding oxygen does nothing for organs that have been petrified."

"How do you dispose of a six-foot-long iguana?" I asked, not sure I really wanted to know the story.

The love of my life sighed. "Well, it's not like you can just throw him out in the trash can. The garbage men probably wouldn't come back. So I decided to bury him."

"Oh. Go on." She was getting pissed now, but that didn't stop me.

"Well, the only way to do it is to dig a six-foot-long trench or a six-foot-deep hole. I opted for the trench. But it was a very hot day, so after three feet I gave up. I thought it would be easy to bend him in half and I'd save myself some labor. Unfortunately rigor mortis had set in, so I had to jump on him to break him to fit him into the trench."

Once my laughter subsided, I smiled at her. "I love you even more than I thought possible."

It was her turn to have wide eyes. "Why? It's a repulsive story!"

I took her hands in mine. "No, it's a great story. It shows compassion in trying to resuscitate him and wanting to give him a proper burial."

"I don't know if jumping up and down on the corpse shows much respect," she said with a frown. "I doubt I could get away with that at work."

"It doesn't matter. I love it. And I love you." There. I'd finally said it. And I was glad I said it. *I love Leonie Doubtfire and her dead iguana!*

Of course, her cell phone chose that moment to ring. For the first time in my life I'd told a woman I loved her. Couldn't she ignore it?

Leonie grabbed her purse and pulled out the cell. She frowned at it for a long time, then, with a stony look, told me she had to leave.

"Whoa! You can't go now. I just told you that I love you!" In spite of my best efforts it came out as a whine. "I've never done that before! This is a major breakthrough for me!" And why didn't she say, *I love you,* back? I'm hardly an expert in these matters, but it does seem like it's a reciprocal thing.

She disappeared into the bedroom without answering and in a few minutes reemerged fully dressed. Leonie kissed me on the cheek. The cheek! What the hell was going on?

"Sorry, Dak. I've got to go." And Leonie

Doubtfire walked out of my condo, leaving me standing there alone, in just my boxers, feeling like an idiot.

As if, these last few months, that was a first for me.

Chapter Twenty-six

"Listen up, maggots. You are not special. You are not a beautiful or unique snowflake. You're the same decaying organic matter as everything else."

—Tyler Durden, *Fight Club*

I didn't hear from Leonie the next day, or the day after that. I wondered if this was what the women who'd dated me before felt like. I didn't like it. It hurt. I left a number of messages on her voice mail, but she never responded. I felt like a washed-up loser.

Louis knew something was wrong, but wisely didn't mention it. Mostly he talked about school, our trip, and his training. I just listened halfheartedly. What could I do? I felt like my heart had been ripped out, then eaten by Magua in *Last of the Mohicans*.

"Dad!" Louis shouted, even though he was standing right in front of me.

"Huh? Oh, hey, buddy. What's up?" I responded glumly.

Louis rolled his eyes. "I'm trying to tell you

that I want to join the Boy Scouts! They have a form you need to sign." He presented me with a form requiring my signature.

"I used to be a Boy Scout," I mumbled, taking the pen he handed me. Maybe this was what Louis needed to give him more of a normal boyhood. Something that could cancel out the assassin training.

After he was asleep I shifted my focus from feeling sorry for myself to my Cub Scout days. I'm pretty sure I liked it. Yes, I know I did. Paris and I were in a den together, and I started to think about campouts, pine wood derbies, and newspaper drives. We always hit bull's-eyes in whatever type of target shooting we did. I think that unnerved the other kids, but since it had been part of our rigorous assassin training, we just shrugged when they asked why we were so good.

I looked at the form. The meeting was next week, and I had to accompany him. Okay. That sounded like something typical fathers did with their typical sons.

I thought about Leonie once more before banishing her from my brain. I didn't need another sleepless night feeling sorry for myself. Instead I went to sleep dreaming of navy blue uniforms, square knots, and trying to remember what the hell Webelos stood for.

Day three found me unwashed, in rumpled

and dirty clothes, sitting in Paris's apartment.

"Let me get this straight. You told her you loved her and you haven't heard from her since?" Paris frowned. "Talk about karma." He shook his head. "I mean, they say 'what goes around comes around,' but, man, this is pure poetic justice."

I stared at him. "Wow. You are *so* supportive."

"Maybe not, but I know irony when I see it." Paris handed me a cup of coffee and sat down.

"So, what do I do now?" Paris might not have been the best person to ask. Don't get me wrong—he'd had his fair share of women. But as far as I knew he'd never fallen in love either.

"I don't know." He shook his head. "She's an odd chick. Not like your normal breed. This one has a brain. Did you say anything to offend her?"

I related the cerulean and dead-iguana stories almost verbatim.

"It's hard to say. Maybe she's got a lot going on at work?"

Now, why didn't I think of that? Of course that was it! Maybe there'd been a mass murder or something and she was up to her neck in dead bodies and their bereaved.

"So, you're saying I should go over there?"

Paris cocked his head to the side. "No, I don't think I said that. If she's busy, you're likely to bother her."

"I should go over there!" I repeated a little louder, with enthusiasm.

"What are you going to do? Start crashing funerals just to see her?"

I jumped up from the couch and hugged Paris. "That is exactly what I'm going to do!"

Even as I showered, shaved, and donned a clean suit, I wondered why I hadn't thought of this before. Of course she was swamped!

Being at Crummy's was a way to demonstrate that I supported her. Leonie would see that and tell me how wonderful I was. It was a foolproof plan.

I pulled into the parking lot, parked, and checked the newspaper. It was the Lutz visitation, and although I'd never met Dean Lutz or any of his family, I was attending his wake.

One final check in the rearview mirror told me that Dak was back. I locked the car and made my way into the funeral home. A different mortician greeted me at the door and sent me to the correct room. The receiving line was short, and I had to play the part.

"I'm so sorry for your loss," I said quietly to the widow.

"How did you know my husband?" she asked through her tears.

235

"Oh." How did I know him? Well, it hardly seemed prudent to say that I had just spotted his visitation notice in the paper today. "I'd met him through work. Just a few times. I didn't know him well but wanted to pay my respects." I thought it was a great cover story. So why, then, was the widow looking at me with her mouth open?

"Could you come with me, please?" Someone tapped me on the shoulder and I saw that it was Leonie. My heart soared as I excused myself from the widow and followed her into the hall.

"What are you doing?" Leonie had her arms folded over her chest. "Are you crashing the Lutz visitation?"

"Yes. I thought I'd come find you, since you've been too busy to return my calls." I said calmly, with only a smidge of defensiveness.

Leonie looked to her right and left before speaking. "That is so wrong, Dak! You can't stalk me like this."

"What are you talking about? I just wanted to show you some support."

"By pretending to be a colleague of Mr. Lutz's? Are you joking?"

"I could be a colleague. How do you know I'm not?" *That's right, boy. Hang on to your dignity!*

"Because Mr. Lutz was the fat man in a circus side show," she said grimly. Okay, she had me there. Come to think of it, the urn *was* enormous (I just thought the widow was being dramatic). And there was that woman with the beard. . . .

"All right, fine! I came here to find you." I pouted.

Leonie sighed and brushed a stray loop of curls from her face, "Look, Dak. I just need some time on my own for a while. Don't call me or stop by. Just give me space."

My jaw was hanging down to my knees. Somehow I managed to close it. "You're . . . you're breaking up with me?"

"It's more complicated than that. Someday I'll explain it to you, but I can't now. Okay?" Leonie patted me awkwardly on the shoulder, then left me alone.

Oh, my God. I just got dumped by a red-headed mortician in a funeral home named Crummy's, after pretending to be a circus freak at the visitation I had just crashed. I was pretty sure there'd be no bouncing back from this.

Chapter Twenty-seven

"I wonder if I have become smaller or has
   the bedroom
Always been the size of a western state.
The aspirin bottle is in the medicine cabinet
Two hundred miles away, a six-day ride,
And my robe hangs from the closet door in
another time zone."

         —Billy Collins, "Saturday Morning,"
         Questions about Angels

"And then she walked out of my life forever. She thought I was a loser and a geek," I said to Paris as I slumped over my scotch at some bar.

Paris raised his eyebrows. "You're quoting movies now? Man, you've got it bad. What is that . . . *Casablanca*?"

"*Ghostbusters*. But that's beside the point." I was on my third drink and starting to realize that this might've been a bad time to take up drinking scotch. But Coney drank scotch, and he was sooooooooo cool. I guess I thought maybe it would rub off on me. But all it was doing was getting me drunk.

Paris shook his head and motioned to the bartender for another Harvey Wallbanger.

"What's up with these fifties girlie drinks, anyway?" I slurred.

"What are you talking about?" Paris asked.

I motioned dramatically toward his glass, "Harvey Wallbangers, Pink Cadillacs, Grasshoppers, and Manhattans. That's what I mean! You had to tell the bartender how to make them! What's next? An Old-fashioned?"

"Ooooh," he replied, "I haven't tried one of them. I'll have that next."

"Dude"—I stabbed a finger at him—"you drink like Zsa Zsa Gabor."

Paris looked pissed. "No, I don't! Frank and Dino and the other Rat Packers drank this stuff!"

I drained my drink and signaled for another. "That was fifty years ago, and they're all dead. Drink something normal!"

"Oh, like you? I've never known you to drink scotch before. A little hung up on Coney?" Paris snorted.

We were stepping out into dangerous territory here. And I was really drunk. If Paris would just quit wiggling like a rubber pencil and stop dividing into two people, I'd let him have it.

"I'd rather emoolate him." I frowned. "Emyoolabe. Emulake."

Paris sighed and rolled his eyes. "Emulate?"

"Right! Instead of a bunch of dead actors." I nodded sharply, which was a mistake, because now there were three Parises.

"All right, Mr. Sunshine. Time to take you home." Paris threw some money onto the bar, and I watched as it got up and danced a jig. He wrestled his arm under me and dragged me out to his car. The whole time I felt as if I were walking through water—upside down.

On the way back home I vaguely remember him calling my mom and asking her to keep Louis overnight and take him to school the next day. I couldn't help smiling. Paris was so responsible. He was not only my wingman, but my son's as well. Why couldn't I be more like that?

"I love you, man," I said to my cousin as he tucked me into bed. Paris rolled his eyes and left me alone in my room, with its spinning ceiling.

I woke up around noon the next day, following a dream where I was being chased around a 1950s casino by Sammy Davis Jr., who was pissed because I accidentally dropped his glass eye into my drink. And let me tell you—he ran like the wind.

Man. I should not *try new alcohol again.* Right. Like it was the scotch's fault. I splashed some more water on my face and looked in the mirror, barely recognizing the gray ghost with purple bags under his eyes.

I was just brushing my teeth for the tenth time when the doorbell rang. I spit quickly, then, grabbing a robe, answered the door.

Paris stood there with a grin and a box of Krispy Kreme doughnuts. "You look like hell."

I snatched the box and nodded. "Yeah, I just got back."

My cousin followed me into the kitchen and started making coffee. "Wait, I know that one." He absently tapped his fingers on his forehead. "It's from *Heathers*, right?"

I nodded. For some reason, lately I could only think in movie quotes. Which was okay, because words had failed me with the only woman I'd ever love. *Oh, brother.*

"Dude," Paris said as he munched on a maple doughnut. "You reek."

"If it weren't for the doughnuts, I'd throw your sorry ass out of here." He was right. I just didn't want to hear it. The huge quantity of scotch I drank was now saturating my pores. There wasn't enough soap in the world to get rid of the smell.

"Well, I've got some news that will cheer you up. Neil came through with the last assassin. He's in Portland, Oregon. I booked us a couple of flights for tonight."

Neil. Neil. My brain scrambled to pin an identity on that name. *Oh, yeah.* Our contact at the CIA. Old friend in college who liked Air Supply. He was helping us nail the National Resources guys.

I opened one eye and squinted at him—mainly because that was all I could manage. "That will cheer me up?" Actually it made me feel worse, as I remembered I'd promised Louis I wouldn't travel so much.

Paris seemed to sense my inner protest. "We're only one more kill away from clearing this assignment. Then you can spend the rest of the year ruminating on how your life has become an ironic tragicomedy."

He rose to his feet and slapped me on the back. It felt like getting hit with a baseball bat and sounded like a sledgehammer hitting concrete. "I'll pick you up at five. Pack for cold, rainy weather. Gin's going to pick up Louis from school and keep him till we get back. *Ciao!*"

I heard the door shut—it sounded like cannon fire. I finished off the pot of coffee and the box of doughnuts, then took a long, hot shower. Maybe Paris was right. Getting this job done would be a huge relief. Leonie could wait. I could win her over again when I got back. At least, I desperately hoped I could.

Somehow I managed to convince myself

that everything would be all right in the end. After all, the Council was likely to give us time off for accomplishing two or three years' worth of work in just under a month. Then I wouldn't have to shuttle Louis between Mom and Gin, and I could get my head straight about Leonie.

Her image came immediately to mind. Leonie's tall and slim body, with her creamy, pale skin and bright, curly red hair. Her face with its elegant, yet elfin features. And those eyes that could turn me into a slave.

But what really caused a lump in my throat was who Leonie was. Funny and smart—she didn't put up with my crap, and seemed to be the only one to see me for who I really was. With a shock I realized that her (considerable) physical attributes came in a distant second to her personality. Another first for me.

But that would have to wait. I opened my suitcase and began to pack for Portland, thinking of how happy Leonie would be when I got back and she realized I really, truly loved her. In this fantasy, Louis went on to cure cancer and win the Nobel Peace Prize— which would be ironic for an assassin.

Chapter Twenty-eight

I'm pretty sure there's a lot more to life than being really, really good-looking. And I plan on finding out what that is.
—Derek Zoolander, *Zoolander*

My head stopped hurting by the time we landed in Oregon. As I stepped off the plane the cool, wet air made me feel a little better. By the time we got to the Super 8 motel I was feeling like my old, brokenhearted self.

"Neil gave us this address." Paris handed me a slip of paper. "He didn't have a name, but I Googled it and found out it's a guy named Fred Costa. He lives alone. Should be pretty easy."

I forced a grin and took another swig of water. My skin tone was starting to come back after the serious dehydration of the night before. I didn't like the bags-under-the-eyes look.

"So," I said, "we go tonight. Let's get this shit knocked out."

We must've been sitting in that rental car for hours, watching Vic's house. It was kind of cute—not at all what I expected for a male assassin, but who knows how people think? I sure didn't have a clue what was going on in Leonie's mind. *Okay, enough of that. Get the job done and then I can get her to tell me what's going on.*

At eleven thirty p.m. the final light went out in Fred's house. Paris and I slipped up to the house a half hour later. Picking the lock on the back door was pretty easy. That was just plain sloppy: A good assassin would be more conscientious of his security. Oh, well, in a few moments it wouldn't matter anyway.

We moved quietly through the house, trying to locate our (hopefully) sleeping Vic. The inside of the house was even more feminine than the outside. Everything in every room screamed that a woman lived there. I whispered my concerns to Paris, but he just shrugged. As we approached the bedroom I prayed silently that there wouldn't be a Mrs. Vic in bed with Fred.

This worry proved needless, as we found him snoring away on a mattress on the floor. Paris pulled out his LED penlight to confirm the kill by locating the Woody Woodpecker tattoo. We'd been so freaked about the last two jobs we wanted to make this one work.

He'd just flashed the light on when I noticed there was no tattoo. Of course, Fred woke up and noticed that there were two men dressed all in black shining a flashlight on him. I aimed my gun at him.

"Who are you? What do you want?" A clearly terrified Vic scrambled to a sitting position, clutching his sheets as if they would protect him against bullets. That was funny.

Paris growled (which made me look at him in surprise). "Are you part of National Resources?"

The man's face screwed up in confusion. "No. What's that?"

"Are you Fred Costa?" I asked in exasperation.

He nodded. "Yeah. Who are you?"

Paris turned to me. "I don't think this is the guy."

I kept my eyes trained on Fred. "He must be the guy. Our source gave us this address. You Googled him, for chrissake."

Paris shook his head. "He doesn't have the tattoo."

I was getting annoyed with this line of conversation. "We didn't check Garth for the tattoo, and we took care of him." I watched Vic to see if the name Garth caused any recognition. But Fred just sat there with a blank look on his face.

"Who the hell is Garth? What tattoo?" Vic whined.

Paris never lowered his flashlight, keeping Vic completely in the dark as to what we looked like. "It's not him," he said simply.

I thought about this for a moment. There was no way I wanted to gun down an innocent man. However, I was just one step away from being able to focus on Louis and Leonie. Family had to come first.

"Don't," Paris said quietly.

Fred was beginning to whimper now. "Is this because of that prank with the donkey and the mayonnaise? Because if it is, I'll never do it again! I promise."

I was just about to ask him what he was talking about when I remembered I was on a job.

"Look!" I shouted at Paris. "Our connection gave us this address. He said this was the place. We can't worry about whether or not he has the right tattoo. Let's finish this and move on!"

I kept the gun leveled and snapped off the safety. The click seemed to drive Vic mad.

"No! Please! It's not me! It's a mistake!" he pleaded. I rolled my eyes. Like I hadn't heard that one before.

"Please!" Vic continued. "It must've been the previous owner! I've only lived here a couple of weeks!" He closed his eyes and flinched, like that would protect him from bullets too.

Paris pushed my arm down. "Wait. Let's hear what he has to say. I really think we might have the wrong guy."

I rolled my eyes and agreed. Paris confirmed the address with Vic, who acted like a condemned man who had gotten a call from the governor at the last minute.

"Yes! That's right." He nodded like a nervous bobble-head doll. "But I just moved here. The house has been on the market a long time. The previous owner moved." A strange look came over his face. "Wait! I still get the other guy's mail! I'll show you!" He started to get out of bed, and I raised the gun again, stopping him midway.

"Just tell us where it is. We'll get it," Paris said calmly.

"Okay! It's on the dining room table. I just sorted it to send back to the post office." A glimmer of hope shone in Fred's eyes. I nodded to Paris, who handed me the flashlight and left to retrieve the mail, while I kept my gun trained on Vic.

This was turning into a major disaster. How did things get so out of hand? Paris and I needed to do more research if this was true. The Council would be pissed if they thought we broke in and almost killed the wrong man.

Paris came back into the room. In the dim light I could make out that he had a stack of bills. These he tossed onto the bed, and Fred greedily snatched them up.

"See!" He held them up to us. "This is what I was talking about!"

Paris took back the flashlight and leaned forward to inspect the mail. Vic scrambled back to what he thought was the safety of the headboard. I watched him with amusement.

"Oh, no," Paris said softly, and I realized we must've had the wrong guy.

"So, who is it? What name is on there?" I asked, the gun still trained on Fred.

Paris snatched up the mail and stuffed it into his coat pocket. "Tell no one of this!" he snarled at the man on the bed. "Tell no one, or we will come back and finish it." Then he dragged me from the room, out of the house, and down to the car.

"Whoa, slow down," I protested. "We don't want to attract attention."

Paris was driving at least forty miles over the speed limit. His face was pale, and he'd broken out in a sweat, which wasn't a good look for him, by the way.

"Hey," I said slowly, trying to be encouraging, "it happens to everybody. Neil didn't know the other guy moved. It's just a simple mistake."

Paris turned and looked at me as if he wanted to say something. In fact, he looked at me longer than I was comfortable with, considering he was driving. He said nothing until we got back to the hotel.

"What the hell was that all about?" I asked as we stripped out of our gear.

Paris looked as if he were going to be sick. Obviously this had affected him more than I thought. Of course he'd be upset. We'd just broken into the home of an innocent man, scared the bejesus out of him, and fled with little or no information on what to do next. Since I was the new, improved, humbled Dak, I tried a different approach.

"It's all right. That guy didn't see us. We'll find the real guy and blow a hole in him"—I held my hands out a foot apart—"this big."

He shook his head, despite my quote from *Parenthood*. Okay. Maybe I should just let him deal with it in his own way. My phone started vibrating on my hip.

"Hey! It's Leonie," I declared. Maybe things were looking up. I flipped the phone open to talk to her.

"Hello?" I asked as casually as I could. Paris started shaking his head vigorously. What a dork. He could at least concede me this small victory. No, he had to muck it all up with his depression about the gig.

"Dak," Leonie began, "I'm so sorry for how I acted at Crummy's. I've been an idiot. I do want to keep seeing you, it's just . . ."

Paris was now doing some kind of charades thing. He was hopping up and down giving me the "kill" sign by dragging his finger across his throat. *Geez*. You'd think our crisis at work could wait till I reconciled with my girlfriend.

"Is this a bad time?" Leonie asked, and I realized I was giving Paris too much of my attention.

I turned my back to him. "No, this is the perfect time. I've been thinking about you a lot and wanted to talk to you." I left out the word *desperately*.

Paris walked over to his coat and pulled the bills from Vic's place out of his pocket. He fairly bounced up to me and tried shoving them under my nose. Couldn't this wait?

I pushed his hand away. "Sorry for my distraction, Leonie. Paris and I are on a job right now, and for some reason he won't leave me"—I shoved him backward onto one of the beds—"alone."

She sighed. It was the most wonderful sound I'd ever heard. "Look, the fact is, there's been some stuff going on in my professional life that I need to reconcile. But I shouldn't have pushed you away like that. You . . . you mean a lot to me, Dakota Bombay. And I want to be with you."

My heart obediently exploded on the spot. I felt as if I were superhuman . . . as if I could fly around the ceiling if I wanted to. "Leonie—that's wonderful! I feel the same way about you. When I get back let's talk. Please?"

She laughed, and I felt a surge of adrenaline. "Of course. Where are you?"

Paris grabbed my phone hand and pulled it back. I thought about killing him on the spot. As I put the cell to my ear again, he shoved the bills right under my nose.

"We're in Oregon—Portland, actually," I said as I finally looked at the envelopes. Time seemed to freeze as I saw the name on the bills of the guy we were supposed to kill.

The phone went dead, and I understood why. Typed neatly across the envelopes was, over and over again, the name Leonie Doubtfire.

Chapter Twenty-nine

"Looks like I picked the wrong week to quit drinking."

—Steve McCroskey, *Airplane*

I slumped to the floor, still holding my cell phone. Paris took it from me and closed it.

"Are you okay?" he asked.

"I don't think so," I said slowly. My voice sounded as if it were really far away—as though I were a demented ventriloquist. Thoughts played bumper cars in my head. *I have to kill my girlfriend. I took an assassin to a family barbecue.* This was the conflict of interest from hell.

This went on for some time, with variations on the same theme. I didn't move from the floor. Eventually, in the background, I felt the shadow of my cousin moving around the room, but I wasn't really aware of anything. Every time I settled on a thought it hurt too much to pursue. Leonie was the enemy. And I was supposed to kill her.

We'd killed her colleagues. I was pretty sure she knew that now. I was also pretty sure it would be difficult for our relationship to bounce back from that.

I became aware that Paris was lifting me off the floor, which was good, because I'd lost all feeling in my ass a long time ago.

"Dak." He shook me gently. "Dak!" He shook a little harder. "Snap out of it, man!"

"Why? Why did it have to be her?"

Paris shook his head. "I don't know. It's a cruel joke. You finally grew up and fell in love, and now you have to kill her. It hardly seems fair."

There was no way out of this. If we failed to complete the mission, the Council would kill us. Those were the rules. Rules I'd grown up believing in. Rules I now wanted to blow up inside a Mickey Mouse costume.

"We don't have to figure this out right now," Paris said, trying to be helpful. "And our plane leaves early in the morning. Let's get some sleep."

He held an open hand out to me. There, on his palm, were two sleeping pills. I took them eagerly. There was no way I could sleep otherwise.

I dreamed I was playing tic-tac-toe with

Leonie. No matter how many times we played neither of us could win. And we couldn't stop playing, because the Council would shoot us if we ended the game. We kept trying different things, but it was no use. Then, just as I came up with a strategy to win the game—one that couldn't possibly exist, I might add—Leonie pulled a gun on me, shooting me six times. As I fell to the floor I said, "Rosebud."

In the morning I was still tired, but not sure it if was residual from the sleeping pills or my bone-crushing depression about Leonie.

"We have to talk about this," Paris said after we went through airport security. "How do we know she isn't waiting outside the airport with a shotgun?"

I froze. I hadn't thought of that. Could she do it? Could she kill me? The answer, though terrifying, filled me with a weird relief: Of course she would. She'd have to do it to save herself. I'd want her to. I envisioned myself gallantly blowing my own head off to save her the agony of doing it herself. My last gift to her. *Ooh.* If they ever made a movie of my life, the most important thing (besides the fact that Matt Damon would play me, of course) would be to include that line.

I shook my head. What was wrong with

me? I didn't want to die. Louis needed me. That little boy shouldn't have to go through losing both his parents so soon.

Another thought popped into my head, making me break out in a cold sweat: What if Leonie tried to kidnap Louis—to make a deal? How well did I really know her, after all? Not well—since I missed the fact that she was an assassin for a competing agency.

"Where are you going?" Paris asked quietly.

I looked around and realized I was walking toward the ticket taker. Only they hadn't called for us to board yet. Sheepishly I sat back down.

"You don't think she'd try to take Louis, do you?" I murmured.

Paris shook his head. "Honestly? I have no idea."

In spite of my cousin's apprehension, I felt ashamed of myself. Leonie wouldn't hurt Louis. But she might kill me out of self-preservation.

Paris said, "I called Liv to pick us up. She's going to have Gin check out the airport to make sure Leonie isn't around." He looked like he wanted to say something else, but changed his mind.

I usually loved flying. We always flew first-class. The hot towel, the comfortable leather seats, more room than the others back in coach. I always reveled a bit in some elitist bastardy. But this flight was agony, because every few minutes and few hundred miles brought me closer to the greatest dilemma I'd faced since they discontinued my signature hair gel a couple of years back.

Part of me hoped Leonie would go into hiding and I'd never see her again. That would solve everything but my broken heart. But if she didn't . . . if she confronted me, would I kill her? The thought of it alone caused an ache that felt like the heartburn I once got after making out with a fire eater (I'm serious).

How could I have missed it? Of course, that was why Leonie got calls to work at odd hours. And the last night we spent together, she'd probably gotten word that she was the only one of the National Resources assassins left. That was why she left so quickly. That was what she meant when she said she had a lot going on professionally. Was she planning on going into hiding and not telling me?

For a moment my heart stopped. Had she been thinking that? Was she just going to drop off the face of the earth, never telling me, leaving me to wonder what the hell happened?

I shook my head to clear it. This wasn't about me. This was about Leonie. She now knew who I was and that I had tried to kill her. Maybe she thought I got involved with her just to keep tabs on her so I could kill her. *Wow.* I really didn't like where this was going.

What the hell was I going to do? I wanted to convince her I wouldn't kill her—that I didn't know who she was when we met, that my feelings for her were genuine. How could I do that? Either she was lying in wait to kill me, or she was gone from my life forever. Either way both of us would be looking over our shoulders for the rest of our lives.

Damn.

Chapter Thirty

"Do I ice her? Do I marry her?"
> —Charley Partana, *Prizzi's Honor*

Gin threw her arms around me as I entered baggage claim. Liv must've told her, I thought dully.

"I'm so sorry," she said over and over again.

I nodded, and in silence the four of us collected our bags and loaded them into Liv's minivan. Liv dropped me off at Gin's house, where I found Louis eating peanut-butter sandwiches.

My heart came alive for the first time in the last twelve hours as my son jumped into my arms.

"I really missed you, buddy," I whispered in his ear.

"I really missed you, Dad," Louis cried out as he squeezed me so hard I saw spots. *Good stranglehold*, I thought proudly.

"I'm really sorry I had to leave. Do you forgive me?"

Louis looked into my eyes—which unnerved me a little bit. "No more travel without me. No matter what. Okay?"

I nodded. I didn't want to be apart from him either. Finally I let him go, and he ran off to play with Romi. Gin offered me a cup of coffee, and I took it gratefully. Sitting there in silence I slowly drained the cup. Gin stood, resting her back against the sink, drinking her own. I realized I was glad to have her with me.

"What should I do?" I asked.

"I don't know, little brother. I wish I did."

Great. No help from her. But at least she was someone to talk to.

"I don't think you and Louis should go home," Gin started carefully. "What if she decides to kill you?"

"If you'd asked me that question last night, I would've said, 'Let her.' But I've got Louis to think about." I drummed my fingers on the table. "I don't think she'll come after me. I think she'll vanish and I'll never see her again."

Gin nodded in response. "I really liked her. I could definitely see her in this family."

"I know. I guess it just wasn't meant to be."

"So, what are you going to do?" Wasn't that the $64,000 question?

"I'm supposed to kill her. That's what I'm contracted to do. Of course, I'm in love with her, so that's not what I'm going to do. I don't know."

Gin said nothing for a moment. It was a definite catch-22, and even my know-it-all sister couldn't solve this one. She changed the subject.

"I showed Louis the basement. He got so excited that I did a little training with him. I hope you don't mind." Last fall she had converted her basement into a child assassin's lair for Romi's and Alta's training.

"He's an amazing kid, Dak. He'll be the best Bombay ever. You should've seen it when he created the beginnings of a dirty bomb using Romi's chemistry set. The kid's got talent."

I smiled at that. Maybe it was my first real smile of the day. Whatever I decided to do, Louis had to remain my first priority.

Eventually Gin convinced me to stay with her. I tucked my son in and told her I needed to go for a drive to clear my head. Gin would've killed me if she knew I was stopping by my condo. But I needed some clothes and wanted to pick up a few things for

Louis. I'd pretty much decided that Leonie would flee rather than confront me. After checking the perimeter outside, I decided it was safe to go in.

I missed Louis. Yes, I knew he was safer with Gin. But it was so weird to walk into my condo alone. Wasn't that the way I'd always wanted it? To be on my own? No ties to anyone? My nightmare scenario was always having to share living space.

Wow. I'd changed, because now the condo just seemed to be as bleak as a cinder-block room. Nothing felt right. I popped my head into the kitchen, hoping to see Leonie making breakfast wearing nothing but my shirt. I entered Louis's room, and instead of wishing it were back to being a guest room, I though it felt so lonely.

Louis wasn't there to roll his eyes when I said something stupid. He wasn't there to make some really strange remark about the exchange rate between the dollar and the euro.

Not knowing what else to do, I flipped on the TV. *Survivor* was on. Instead of grabbing a beer and relaxing, I felt a sudden urge for Kool-Aid and popcorn. Louis thought I should buy something healthier for him to drink. Hell, I thought all kids wanted colored sugar water.

I switched the television off. I threw some things in a bag. What a mess.

A few short months ago my life was perfect. Or so it seemed. I didn't have to get up early every morning to get my son off to school. I had my pick of women to keep me company every night. No one told me I couldn't do this or eat that because I now had a son.

I was lying to myself. I wanted my kid here on the couch with me. I wanted Leonie back in my bed. I wanted to take Louis to school and pick him up. And I wanted to crash funerals just to get a glimpse of that lovely redhead.

The phone rang and I pounced on it, hoping it was my son calling to say good night.

"I need to ask you something." Leonie's voice was chilling.

"Anything. Come over," I pleaded.

"No."

"Okay. I'll come over to your place. Or to Crummy's."

"No, not there." She paused for what seemed like a millennium. "Meet me at 1224 Adams Street." She hung up before I could ask anything more.

Well, she wanted to meet me. That was at least something, I told myself as I pulled into the parking lot of a local farm equipment manufacturer. I was surprised to see the lights on and machines running this late. Then I remembered that this was how two of the *Terminator* movies ended and suppressed a shudder.

"Leonie?" I called out. And then I noticed that while everything was running, there were no people anywhere. Was she going to kill me here? This really was like *The Terminator*. But was she the wuss Linda Hamilton, or the buff Linda Hamilton?

She appeared about ten feet away and made no move to come any closer. I wanted to close the gap, but was afraid that might look too threatening, so I stood still.

"I can't believe you stalked me and used me like that," Leonie shouted over the din. "I thought you really loved me."

"I do love you. I didn't know that you were on my hit list!" *Please believe me.*

"How can I believe you? Why should I?"

I thought about that for a moment. It was understandable. I'd feel the same way. *Damn.* That wouldn't make this any easier.

"I don't know how to convince you other than to tell you that you're the only woman I've ever loved. If I thought you were an assassin, would I have let you get so close to Louis? My family? Jesus, Leonie! They all love you!"

She paused for a moment, and I could see that she was thinking about it. I couldn't even imagine what was going on under all that red hair.

"I'm sorry, Dak." She was frowning. "I have to go. If you're lying, then this is the best thing for me. If you're telling the truth, then it's the best thing for you." She shrugged. "Don't you see that?"

I charged her, determined to hold her down until she listened. There was a loud bang behind me and I turned to look. When I turned back, Leonie was gone.

Chapter Thirty-one

"I can't seem to face up to the facts
I'm tense and nervous and I can't relax."
——"Psycho Killer," Talking Heads

I found myself drowning my sorrows at a bar. Actually it was Algonquin's Table, a place I used to come to pick up blondes. I'm not sure why I went there tonight. Maybe it was the first place I saw on my way home.

"You look unhappy." A petite blonde pulled up a stool next to mine and ordered a chablis.

I didn't respond.

"Hey," she purred. "What's your name?"

I turned to her, intending to blow her off. She was cute. No, she was smokin' hot. Big brown eyes, long, thick blond hair, and a body you usually had to pay a lot of money to get.

"Dakota. And you are?" I wasn't sure why I responded.

"Eva. Nice to meet you, Dakota." She was

really on the make. Five months ago she'd already be in my bedroom by now, doing things she never thought physically possible. Did I miss those days?

She chatted about absolutely nothing—to which I didn't respond. It was pretty obvious she was looking for a good time. The old Dak wouldn't have passed up an opportunity like this. And since Leonie was gone forever and I was lonely for the first time in my life, the old Dak was all I had left. Eva kept working me over—trying to get an invitation to my place. I ignored her, threw some money on the bar, and left.

Unfortunately I'd realized that the bag with my and Louis's clothes was still back at the condo, and worse, Eva followed me home and forced her way past me as I unlocked the door. I was so numb with missing Louis and Leonie that I didn't even have the energy to try to stop her.

"This is nice," she said. Turning to face me in the living room, she kissed me. Eva smelled really good, but my body wasn't in any hurry to rise to the bait.

"Mind if I use the powder room?" she purred.

Powder room? Leonie would never call it that. She'd make fun of anyone who said something like that, and I would laugh.

"Sure. Down the hall to your right."

While Eva was in the bathroom I tried to figure out how to get rid of her. This chick was seriously pissing me off, and I wanted her gone so I could go back to Gin's and Louis. After what seemed like a long time Eva came back.

She pushed me to the couch and climbed onto my lap, her lips on mine. I pushed her off of me and scrambled to my feet.

"What's wrong?" She pouted.

"This party is over," I said, pointing to the front door.

"You don't really want me to go, do you?"

I nodded. I really wanted her to go.

"What's your story, Dakota?"

"No story. Just a guy. Nothing big." *Wow*. Not only was the old Dak gone, he apparently had undergone a lobotomy. *Huh*. Lobotomy sabbatical.

"I just want to get to know you better." Eva reached for my hand.

"Look," I started, "don't get me wrong, but I'm just not interested." Oh, my God! Who was that guy? Why was he turning down sex from a hot blonde? In the old days he would've told any one of a hundred lies just to get her in the sack.

There was a flash of anger in her eyes, but

she quickly hid it. This chick was kind of scary.

"Let me guess—you just broke up with someone. Is that it?" Eva's voice regained its purr. "Maybe I can help you forget about her for a little while."

She started kissing me, and I pushed her back. "No. I don't think so."

"Well, why don't you just close your eyes and pretend I'm her?" Eva started kissing my neck, her hand reaching between my legs.

"Only if you have a Woody Woodpecker tattoo," I muttered—I thought—to myself.

"I don't work for National—" She sat up sharply, recognizing her mistake.

I grabbed her wrist. No tattoo. But she knew something. Eva scrambled to her feet and pulled a gun from a thigh holster. Now, why didn't I feel that earlier? Seemed to me I should have. Of course, I'd been too busy playing with alliteration. *Idiot.*

"Dammit. They told me you were partial to blondes!" Her eyes burned. "I dyed my hair for this gig. Now I have to do this the hard way."

I stood only a few feet away from her. I'd have the advantage if I charged. The old Bombay family nursery rhyme popped into my head: "Rush a gun, run from a knife."

"Who are you?" I asked calmly, as if a gun weren't pointed at my chest.

"Never mind!" She fairly spit the words out. *Wow.* This bitch could go from zero to psycho in ten seconds. "Shit! Shit!" she cursed herself.

"Look." My thoughts raced, and I wondered if Leonie had sent her. Maybe National Resources had more than just five players? No, she said she didn't work for them. "What is it you want? Maybe I can help."

"Doc Savage needs something from you. I don't want to hurt you. I just need some files. Then I'll go."

I exploded. "I'm so sick of this Doc Savage bullshit! And if you didn't want to hurt me, why send those men after me? And why the gun now? What goddamned files do you want?"

Eva actually smirked. "I need the gun because you're supposedly dangerous. And I don't know which files. I was just supposed to knock you out and let this guy in once you were unconscious. He'd look for the files and then we'd be out of here."

I shook my head. "Why are you telling me all of this?"

"I *don't know*! I've never done this before!" She started screaming and, forgetting she had a perfectly good weapon in her hand, picked up a book from the end table and threw it at me.

I dodged it neatly (I'm not a total loser), then dove for Eva and the gun. It took me only a few seconds to subdue her. She was telling the truth. She really hadn't done this before.

I managed to handcuff her by the ankles and wrists to one of the kitchen chairs.

"What time was this Doc Savage coming by, anyway?"

"One hour. He'll be here in one hour." The fight had pretty much gone out of our girl. I didn't push it. Whoever was in charge would be here soon, and then I'd find out what was going on.

In the meantime I had a couple of cups of coffee to wake up so I could think. Eva wasn't much use to me as a conversationalist, so I ignored her.

None of these Doc Savage attacks made any sense. They all seemed to focus on wanting something in my home. Well, except for the dude in the men's bathroom. Eva said they didn't want to hurt me, just wanted some files. What kind of files? I wasn't much of a paperwork guy. I didn't really have any use for it. Paris, on the other hand, kept everything all the way back to his first tooth.

No matter how many times I thought about

it, it didn't make any sense. If the Council wanted something from me, they'd just send Grandma and her Uzi. Leonie was the only one left from National Resources. And I was pretty sure she was long gone.

All I knew was that I'd had too much coffee and had a full bladder. I stood and winked at Eva and headed to the bathroom. After a few moments of relief I stepped into my hallway and felt a sharp, sudden pain at the back of my head. There was another blow before I could turn around, and everything went black.

Imagine my surprise when I woke up alive (and just wishing I were dead) and in pain on the floor. A large knot on the back of my head indicated the how. And a bent fireplace poker on the floor demonstrated the what. I staggered from room to room searching for the why.

My condo had been ransacked. Drawers hung open like astonished mouths, their contents all over the floor. Cushions were everywhere but on the furniture, and my clothes had attempted to make a break for it from my closet.

To my shock, nothing was damaged. I hadn't expected that. There was a huge mess, but nothing was ripped or broken. Of course,

Eva was gone. But I was pretty sure she hadn't done this on her own.

Without knowing what else to do, I called Paris. He came over and helped me clean everything up.

"It's got to be associated with National Resources," Paris said. "You said this chick mentioned them. Who else would it be?"

I picked up the last spoon from the kitchen floor. Man, those were some nice spoons. I didn't even remember where I got them, but they were really nice.

"Dak."

"Oh, sorry." I shoved the flatware into the drawer. "I'm still a little dizzy from the two blows on the head."

"I think we need to tell the Council about everything."

I looked up sharply. "What? No! They'll insist I kill Leonie. I can't do that."

"May I remind you that you've had three attacks—two in your own home? It isn't safe to bring Louis back here until we close out this deal."

My perfect posture slumped. "I didn't think about that."

"And it looks like the NR guys have more resources than we thought. Maybe we just can't get them all by ourselves."

Leonie or Louis. That was what it came down to. "I can't do it." I shook my head. "I can't sic the Council on Leonie."

Paris put his hand on my shoulder. "Maybe they won't go after her. I mean, they gave Gin a reprieve. After what they put you through last time, maybe they'll let her off the hook?"

I looked at my cousin for a long time. He'd never hurt me. And I had to take care of Louis. It was a long shot, but I had to try.

Paris stood up and pulled his cell phone out. "I'll do it. You go clean yourself up."

I nodded, grateful to have him handle things. Paris definitely had a cooler head. If anyone could manage to pull this off, it would be him.

Of course, no one was answering the bat phone on Santa Muerta. It was two a.m. here, which would make it . . . Oh, hell, my head hurt too much to calculate the time difference. Paris sent me to bed and insisted on sleeping on my couch, just in case. Good man. He was always someone you could really depend on. A dependable assassin.

I woke midafternoon to find Paris in the kitchen making eggs and bacon. What a guy!

"Any news?" I asked, not really wanting an answer.

"I talked to Dela this morning. She was going to call an emergency Council meeting for"—he paused and looked at his watch—"right about now." He pushed a plate of scrambled eggs, hash browns, and bacon toward me. "Might as well eat."

The food was excellent. I didn't realize Paris could cook. We said nothing as we ate. Both of us were probably thinking the same thing, coming up with no answers. I finished quickly and decided on a shower.

While I felt clean and full afterward, I also felt numb. Leonie's breakup had devastated me more than the attack last night. And now Louis was in jeopardy. I toweled off, feeling nothing but despair, and pulled on a pair of jeans and a black T-shirt.

I walked into the living room just in time to see Paris ending a conversation on his cell. My heart lurched. The moment of truth.

Paris winced as he hung up his cell. "Well, I guess you are off the hook on this dilemma."

"Is the Council calling off the hit on Leonie? That's great! Now I just have to find her and convince her everything's going to be all right!" I jumped up and hugged my cousin.

But Paris pushed me away. "No. That's not it. Grandma doesn't want you to have to hunt the woman who made you grow up. She still feels bad about almost killing you last year."

I frowned. "That's good news, isn't it?"

"They still want her dead."

His words sank slowly into my skin, ending in a pool of ooze around my ankles. "Oh, no," I whispered. "No." I said more forcefully, using the anger that welled up in my throat. "That's not going to work. I can't let them do that."

Paris nodded, as if he'd known this was going to be my reaction all along. "All right. I'm in this with you. Let's go get her."

"Really? You'd come with me?" I couldn't believe it.

He grinned. "Hey, if there's no hope for you to have a chance at true love, then I'm screwed."

I slapped him on the back. Maybe he drank sissy drinks and wrote poetry. Maybe he was anal-retentive and wore silly pajamas. But he was still my wingman.

"How do we find her?" I asked.

Paris thought for a few moments, then smiled. "Why don't we call Missi?"

Chapter Thirty-two

"We've got a blind date with Destiny—and it looks like she's ordered the lobster."
—the Shoveler, *Mystery Men*

It turned out that Missi was at a technology convention in Vegas. She agreed to meet with us, so Paris and I made plans to hop a red-eye, meeting her in her room about one a.m.

"What are you doing?" Louis had his arms folded over his chest as he watched me pack.

"What are you doing up? You have school!"

"I'm going with you." He added a frown to his stance, appearing very menacing for a six-year-old.

I sat down next to him, ignoring Paris, who was tapping his wristwatch to tell me we had to leave.

"You can't go with me. It's going to be very dangerous. Remember when I told you what we do for a living? Well, there are some dangerous people out there chasing Leonie. Paris and I are going to find her and bring her back."

"You promised you wouldn't leave without me!" This time he stamped his little foot.

"Louis, I know I promised that. But taking you would mean putting you in danger. And I just can't do that. You are too important to me. I need you to stay here with Gin and Diego until I get back."

My son didn't look convinced. But there was no way I was taking him with me. Losing Leonie would be devastating. Losing Louis would kill me.

"I'm an awful father for breaking this promise, I know. But I love you so much it hurts. And if anything happened to you I would never, ever forgive myself. You are my son, and I need you to stay here." I put on what I thought was a very convincing stern-father face.

Louis exploded into tears and threw himself into my arms. I held him while he cried, trying desperately not to sob myself. After a few minutes I took him by the shoulders.

"You need to stay here and help Gin take care of everyone. Okay? I'll be back. I promise. And I'll never leave you again—unless you want me to."

Louis sniffled and wiped his eyes on his

sleeve. "Okay, Dad. But you'd better come back."

I nodded, and Paris and I left. I spent the next two hours on the plane fighting back the tears.

We found Missi as soon as we landed. It took only about half an hour to fill her in on everything.

"Let's see what we've got." Missi pulled out the weirdest-looking laptop I'd ever seen and began to turn it on.

"What is that?"

Missi grinned like a kid in a chocolate playroom. "Do you like it? It's my latest thing."

Paris and I looked at each other, then turned back to the computer. It was about the size of any other notebook, but it had all kinds of weird attachments and wires sticking out of it. Closed, it resembled the kind of sandwich a robot would eat. Once it was opened I could see that the monitor was really four small screens, and the keyboard had ten rows of keys instead of the usual six.

"Holy cow." Paris whistled under his breath.

"How does it work?" I asked a little louder.

Missi smiled. "I guess you could say it works like a laptop. It's just tricked out to my specs. With four screens I can multitask more efficiently. This puppy has infrared capability, satellite feeds to U.S., European, and Asian government space programs, and the best GPS system I could put together."

She touched the keyboard and the thing quivered to life. "I added some special touches to the keyboard to make work easier. Each monitor is color-coded, and I just switch back and forth between them using the touchpad."

I held my hand up to interrupt. "Okay, it's totally cool. But let's just get to the part about how we can find Leonie before Doc Savage, National Resources, or the Council does."

Missi had the good grace not to look crushed that I interrupted. I figured Paris would ask her more about it later, but Leonie's life hung in the balance.

"Sorry. I just get carried away sometimes," she said. "I can't take stuff like this to the convention."

"My bad, Missi. I'm being insensitive." This caused her to jerk her head toward me in surprise. Apparently I wasn't shocking just my immediate family with my personality makeover these days.

"Wow," she said. "No, no, you're right. We have to find your girlfriend before anyone else does." She began typing on the weird keyboard. "Give me everything you know about her."

I told her that her family ran a funeral home in Oregon, and it didn't take long to find the Doubtfire Funeral Home in Portland. Missi plugged a green wire from the keyboard into the monitor as the funeral home came up on screen number one. When I raised my eyebrow she told me she'd hacked into their security system. I filled her in on everything I knew about Leonie, from Crummy's to current and former addresses to physical description.

Missi kept working, plugging wires in and tapping on the keyboard, until all four screens showed different aspects from Leonie's life.

"Here"—Missi pointed at the first screen— "I'm tapping into her family's home and work phone lines. I can actually get recordings of conversations past and present. No future ones though. But I'm working on it."

How the hell could she do that?

"This monitor shows her current home and cell phone lines. I can tap into those too. I can access them as far as three days ago. That should give us some info on where she's planning to hide out.

"And this"—she grinned broadly—"is a GPS tracking program. I've typed in her name, description, phone numbers, and Social Security number. I should have her located in no time."

I slumped to the bed, my head whirling. Paris looked like he'd been hit with a Taser.

"Does the Council know you have this technology?" he asked weakly.

"Hell, no. Nobody knows—not even Mom. I think Monty and Jack suspect something, though, because once when they said they were at the library I tracked them to this kegger in Belize—"

"Missi!" I shouted.

Her face went from dazed back to the present. "Oh. Right. Anyway, I just want you to know that I understand what you're going through, so that's why you now know about Lulu."

"Lulu?" I asked, afraid of the answer.

"That's what I named her. Oh!" A buzzing noise emanated from Lulu, and she turned toward it. "Found her! Well, that's weird."

Hearing Missi say that something was weird was truly a strange experience.

"She's here. In Vegas. Huh," Missi said distractedly.

"Are you serious?" That *was* weird. "Where is she? And is anyone following her?"

She pulled up another screen. "It looks like she's"—Missi looked at us with an odd expression—"in the room next door. On the left."

I ran to the door that adjoined that room to

Missi's. Knocking was out of the question. Leonie would just run away again. So I scrambled through my pockets to find some way to pick the lock.

Missi appeared beside me, rolling her eyes. She held what looked like a garage door opener and pushed the red button. After a few seconds the door popped open.

"I need one of those!" I said as I burst through both sets of doors to find a shocked Leonie looking out the window.

"What the . . ." She opened her mouth, then shut it. "How did you . . . ?"

I closed the gap between us and crushed her to me.

"Oh, my God," I said over and over. "You're all right. You're all right."

"Dak," Leonie murmured against my shoulder. "Dak! I won't be all right if you don't stop crushing me!"

I loosened my grip but did not let go. "You're not going anywhere until you hear what I have to say."

Paris entered the room, gesturing madly and whispering, "In here! Get in here!"

I dragged Leonie into Missi's room, and Paris shut and locked both doors behind us.

"Hi! I'm Missi, Dak's cousin. You must be Leonie."

Leonie cautiously reached out and took Missi's hand.

"What the hell is going on here?" she asked.

I started to talk when Paris brought his finger to his lips. "Someone with a gun is on the elevator. He'll be here any minute," he whispered.

"How do you know that?" Leonie whispered to me, and I shushed her. I wanted to know that too, but figured Missi's Lulu could do a lot more than I thought.

Missi sighed and pulled a case out from under the bed. Inside were six semiautomatic handguns, all .45s. We snatched them up, quietly shoving magazines into them and racking the slides.

We couldn't hear anything at first. Then there was a rap on the door to Leonie's room. I looked around and realized we were pretty much trapped. Our best defense would be to wait out whoever it was.

It seemed like hours passed before we heard the door open next door. I gripped my gun tightly. Whoever it was took this assignment seriously. Of course he'd break into her room. He had no idea we were just on the other side of the wall. Missi told us she'd used a fake name on the hotel register.

There was the usual sound of movement in the room. I heard drawers opening and closing, the shower curtain rustling. This bastard was looking everywhere.

A thought chilled me: What if he decided to stay and ambush Leonie? How long could we hold out in silence next door? If we tried to leave through the hallway, what if he decided to leave at that moment too? *Damn.*

So we sat. Missi quietly showed Paris more of Lulu, while Leonie and I sat together on the bed.

"Who's in my room?" she whispered.

"I don't know," I replied, wondering how much to tell her. If I was ever going to gain her trust, it was now. "I'm just glad I found you before he did." I neglected to add the word *seconds* before *he did*, but she got the idea.

Leonie looked at me with an expression I couldn't read. Hopefully it was, *Wow, Dak! You saved me from your own family! You do love me!* But I couldn't tell. We just sat there.

I came out of distraction hearing a strange noise on the other side of the adjoining door. I recognized it immediately. The uninvited guest next door was sliding his hands around the door, trying to decide whether Leonie was in here. I turned to Missi and shrugged. She frowned and picked up the phone.

"Yes, security?" she asked, using a very loud, high-pitched Southern accent. "This is Myra Hodges in six-one-one-one. I think someone has broken into the room next door and I'm mighty worried. Could you send someone up immediately?"

I looked back toward the door. The sound had stopped. In fact, it sounded as if he were leaving. I ran to the door and looked through the security window as a blurred figure in a dark hooded sweatshirt ran toward the stairwell and disappeared. He was gone too fast for me to ID him.

Now, I want you to know that you should never look through those things. Most assassins love to use them to shoot you through the eyeball—which is really gross but totally effective.

"Good thinking." I gave Missi the thumbs-up as I heard security running down the hall.

Missi just waved me off modestly. "That was kid stuff."

Paris tucked his gun into the back of his jeans. "So, what now? Whoever it is could just be lying in wait in the stairwell."

"He won't be on the elevators, and he won't show up in the hallway until security is gone next door." I looked at Leonie. "We have to go. Now."

Missi winked at me. "Good luck!"

I nodded, shoved the gun into my waistband, and pulled my jacket down over it. Leonie lifted her dress and shoved her gun into a thigh holster. I started to salivate. That was so hot.

She nodded and the three of us slipped through the door toward the elevators. It seemed like a very long time before the doors opened. Paris got on and immediately started hitting the CLOSE DOOR button.

The elevator turned out to be slower than the damned train at Disney World. And it played "The Girl from Ipanema" in Muzak. I looked at Paris and saw that he was mouthing the lyrics. That was it. I'd have to plan an intervention for him once we got home.

Chapter Thirty-three

"Over? Did you say 'over'? Nothing is over until we decide it is! Was it over when the Germans bombed Pearl Harbor? Hell, no!"
—Bluto, *Animal House*

It took only a few minutes to grab a cab outside, and with no small measure of relief the three of us sighed as the taxi drove us across town to the airport.

"We're flying out of here?" Leonie frowned as I paid the driver and sent him away.

I shook my head. "No. We're renting a car here to drive to Reno. We'll fly from there."

We didn't say much at first. Paris drove, pretending to be more interested in the road than anything else. I sat in the back with Leonie because I was afraid she'd jump out at any minute.

"So," I started, "are you convinced about my feelings for you yet? I'd never kill you, Leonie."

She looked away from me, out the window

for a moment. Then she turned and looked me straight in the eyes.

"Where are we going?"

The truth was, I hadn't quite figured that out yet. Taking her home was dangerous. Sooner or later the Council would guess I had her and come get her. Also, until I had this mess with Doc Savage cleared up, I didn't want to put her in danger. As far as National Resources went, there was no way of knowing whether someone was coming for her.

"First there's something I need to know." Okay. I was stalling. "Does the name Doc Savage mean anything to you?"

"The Man of Bronze? I read those books when I was a kid. Why?"

My heart jumped a little when I discovered we had something more in common. "Nothing else? Nothing more . . . current?"

Leonie shook her head. "No."

"Is there anyone else involved with National Resources? Someone still alive?"

Her eyes narrowed. "Why would I tell you that? You killed the others."

She had a point.

"I didn't know you were involved, I swear." I did a little cross-my-heart thingie.

"If you had known about me from the beginning, would you have killed the other four?" Her chin was set in the most adorable look of defiance.

"How can I answer that? I don't know." It wasn't much, but it was the truth. "Were they friends? Did you know them well?" I was worried about her answer.

"No. I never knew who they were. We were supposed to operate in a vacuum. There's a handler who kept tabs on us. She's the one who called when the last one before me bought it." She handed me her phone and I saw the message: *Number four dead. Run and hide.*

"Who's the handler?" I asked.

"There's a handler?" Paris echoed from the driver's seat. So he was listening after all.

Leonie waved me off. "Don't worry. She never did anything but negotiate the jobs and assign them. I don't know anything about her. She'll just go into hiding and never be heard from again. She's not a threat."

I relaxed at hearing that, but still wondered if this woman was Doc Savage. And if there was a handler, were there other employees? Leonie must have received assignments from the handler. Or were there others involved? Others who might at this very minute be hunting us?

"So, what happens now?" Leonie asked.

I looked out the window at the desert.

Frankly, I had no idea. Once we got to Reno maybe we should hole up for a while. At least until we could convince the Council that Leonie was no longer a threat and solve the Doc Savage problem.

"Why did you get into this business, anyway?" I asked. "It's dangerous. What were you thinking?"

She laughed. There was a hard edge to it. "Christ, Dak. I was an English major. The only thing I had to look forward to after college was running a funeral home. I was recruited. It kind of made sense, considering the business I was in."

Grabbing her arm, I pulled up the sleeve. No tattoo. "Why don't you have the tattoo?"

"That stupid thing? What? Are you joking?" When she saw that I wasn't, Leonie continued. "I refused to get it." She rolled her eyes. "Like I'd put Woody Woodpecker on my arm. The company backed down once they realized I didn't need a cartoon on my arm in order to kill people."

After a moment she spoke again. "I thought I'd be working for the government. You know, saving the world. It turned out they'd lied to me. I was trying to figure out how to quit when I met you."

I must've looked somewhat unconvinced, because she continued. "I'm serious. I wanted out. I guess in a weird way . . . you are helping me."

I realized I'd never spoken to anyone outside the family about the trade. And I'd never met anyone who became an assassin by choice. Still, we had something strangely in common: We both worked in family businesses that dealt with death, and we were both assassins.

"What about you?" she asked. "Why are your cousins involved?"

Paris caught my glance in the rearview mirror. He shrugged. I took that to mean he didn't care if I told her. But there was a problem—Bombays aren't allowed to tell outsiders anything about what we do. I could understand that. Imagine how many of us would be in prison via a bad breakup.

On the other hand, if we survived this I planned to make Leonie part of the family. You weren't supposed to tell your significant other until the ink was dry on the marriage certificate. Well, this was an exception to the rule, I decided. So I launched into the history of the Bombay family. By the time we got to Reno Leonie's eyes were huge.

"That's pretty wild," she said. "I knew we had rivals, but I didn't realize how, um, bizarre they were." She squinted at the mountains in the distance. "Wow. A private island. Cool."

"Let's stop here," Paris suggested as he pulled into a nondescript hotel parking lot.

I nodded in agreement and watched as Paris went inside to get a room. He returned in a few minutes with a key, and the three of us made it to the room.

Paris cased the room for security problems, and I looked around. We had nothing. No luggage, no personal belongings. Hell, Leonie didn't even have her purse. But we were still alive. That had to count for something.

Paris immediately called and ordered pizza delivery. Leonie sipped a Diet Coke and watched as I paced the room nervously.

"I don't know who's following us, but I do know that we have to convince the Council that Leonie's not a threat to us," I said more to myself than anyone.

"How can we do that?" Paris asked.

"I don't know. I could go to Santa Muerta and plead her case."

"You can't leave Leonie alone," Paris answered.

"Guys! I'm not exactly helpless, you know," Leonie interrupted. "Hello, I have a lot of kills under my belt."

I thought about asking her how many, but

decided my ego was too fragile for me to know the answer to that.

"Well, they let Diego live when he came to the island as a stranger," Paris mused.

He was right. Diego had accompanied our raid on the Council last year, and that was a huge violation of the rules. No nonfamily member ever saw Santa Muerta. Alive, that is.

While it was true that the Council had made an exception for Gin's sake, I didn't trust them to do it again. We needed the Council's support on this matter. Since I didn't know who the hell was after us (and at this point there were a couple of suspects), the only safe place for Leonie was Santa Muerta. *Huh.* That was ironic. The island was either the most dangerous or the safest place on earth for her.

I snapped my fingers. "I've got it! We'll get married!" I thought it was a great idea. So why did Paris look so dubious and Leonie so nauseated?

"Leonie, would you marry me?" I asked her urgently.

"This isn't exactly what I had in mind when I dreamed of a proposal." She didn't look happy. Why didn't she look happy?

"Well," I said, "I love you. And Louis loves you. And everyone in my family thinks you're amazing."

Leonie just stared at me. "So you're serious? You aren't just proposing so you can save my life?"

That seemed like an odd question. "Don't you feel the same way about me?" I begged.

She was taking too long to answer. *Holy shit!* What if she didn't love me?

"Yes, Dak. I do love you. I adore your son and family." She shrugged. "I just didn't really picture it all going down this way."

Paris grabbed the phone book. "There are three chapels within a five-mile radius of this hotel. Let's go."

After calling the front desk and asking them to pay for and hold on to the pizza until we got back, we climbed in the car and drove to the first chapel on the list.

I'd seen chapels with Elvis impersonators, Elvira impersonators, and the like. What I'd never seen was a chapel with a *Star Trek* theme. A very fat Captain Kirk look-alike in full regalia welcomed us onto the deck. The organist somewhat resembled a badly aged Uhura.

Mr. Spock performed the ceremony. I could handle the part where he did the thing with his hand and said, "Live long and prosper," but when he concluded the ceremony with, "This union is logical," I had to smother a laugh. Then Tribbles fell from the ceiling. I kid you not. I handed two hundred dollars to the organist, ignoring her weird eye tic, and we fled. The whole thing took maybe fifteen minutes.

Stunned and a little freaked out, Leonie and I stumbled out of the *Star Trek* chapel and into married life. I crushed my wife to my chest while Paris waved our marriage certificate in the dusty, arid wind to dry it.

A shot rang out, and the three of us dove behind the row of parked cars. Scrambling to a crouched position I reached for my bride, only to find her in a very hot combat position, aiming her gun at the alley behind us. *Damn.* She looked amazing. I sat down in the gravel and stared, glassy-eyed, at the woman of my dreams as she silently swept the alley and gave us a thumbs-up.

Another shot broke my daze, and I regained my composure, creeping around the first car to check out the lot. Nothing seemed to be out of place. In fact, there were no concerned pedestrians or police sirens wailing in the distance.

Leonie appeared beside me. "It must've been a car backfiring."

Paris nodded his agreement and we rose, holstering our weapons. We climbed in the car and drove off, circling numerous city blocks along the way to make sure we weren't followed.

"Wow," I said to Leonie. "You looked hot back there."

She turned to me with a strange look. "You've seen women do this before, right? Your mom and sister are assassins. Isn't that what you said?"

"Yes, but they never looked as good as you did just now."

"Oh, for christ's sake, Dak. Don't turn me into a sexist fantasy or I'll have the marriage annulled."

What could I do? I nodded sheepishly and turned my attention to the road.

"I never thought I'd see the day you'd get married." Paris still looked a little shocked as we ate pizza back in our room. "And don't even think of consummating it tonight. Wait until you get a little privacy. Please."

Leonie tore another can from the six-pack that came with the pizza. "I can't believe it either. I always had the traditional idea of a full wedding. Not a quickie on the deck of the starship *Enterprise*." She giggled and I melted.

It was almost as if our troubles were gone. I watched as she popped open her can. Everything she did seemed elegant. She deserved better than this.

A strange fizz came from the can Leonie opened. Blue smoke started to pour out of it, and she dropped it to the ground. Paris threw a towel over it, but it was too late. My whole body felt as if it were swaying. I watched as Leonie collapsed onto the bed and Paris fell on top of her. I would have protested that arrangement had I not already hit the floor.

Chapter Thirty-four

"A prayer's as good as a bayonet on a day like this."

—Color Sergeant Bourne, *Zulu*

Ever have one of those days when you get married by a Vulcan in a *Star Trek*–themed chapel while on the lam in Nevada and wake up tied to a chair with your new wife and best friend in a strange room, your grandma standing over you with a .38?

Well, this was one of those days. I came to tied rather uncomfortably to a chair. My pain was forgotten the minute I saw that Leonie was in the same situation on my right, Paris on my left. I didn't recognize the room. In fact, I had no idea if we were still in Nevada or on Santa Muerta. If the latter, this room was new.

The walls were a blindingly stark black-and-white tile, as was the floor. It was a very uncomfortable room. Leonie was still uncon-scious, but Paris was awake. Grandma stood in front of us, a brushed-steel .38 in the shoulder holster she wore over her muumuu. There was no sign of anyone else in the room.

"What's going on?" I said with more than a little attitude. This was the second time in one year my grandmother had threatened me, and I was getting pissed off.

"I should be asking you the same thing, Dakota." She looked angry.

"I suppose the Council is going to take ac-tion on the job?" I was really being an ass-hole, but this was irritating.

"Actually"—Grandma tilted her head to one side—"they don't know you're here yet. I did this myself. I wanted to find out what the hell you were doing before Lou killed you."

Okay, so that was good news. Maybe I'd better wise up.

"I can't let the Council kill Leonie. I love her."

Grandma looked at Leonie. "She's the one who made a man out of you? Hell, she should get a Nobel Prize for that." She laughed. "She's really lovely, Dakota. But that's beside the point now, isn't it?"

"Where are we?" Paris asked, which was good, because if he continued to remain silent I'd deck him. Not that I could. But I would.

"Let's just say you're safe for now. I have a

safe room in my apartment. It's soundproof, and no one knows about it. Until now, that is."

"Jesus, Grandma," Paris cursed. "At least untie us if you aren't going to turn us over to the Council."

"Yeah!" I backed him up. "This is stupid. You aren't going to kill us."

She arched her right eyebrow, and for a moment she reminded me of Leonard Nimoy. "Oh? I'm not? Are you sure?"

"I am so sick of this family," I muttered. No one else had to deal with family shit like this.

"Quit pouting!" Grandma barked. "This is serious. You are in big trouble."

Paris snorted. "Then just shoot us. Because I'm so over these dramatics."

Okay, right attitude, wrong choice of words. "Grandma, you aren't going to kill us and you aren't going to hand us over to the Council, so just untie us."

Leonie started to stir. She opened her eyes and immediately summed up the situation as bad, and possibly bizarre.

Grandma softened. "Hello, dear. It's so nice to meet the woman who tamed my idiot grandson. You must be very special." She smiled and patted Leonie's shoulder.

Leonie shot me a what-the-fuck? look. It was strange. But if we lived, she'd eventually get used to the quirks of the Bombays.

"So, Lou, Troy, and the others don't know we're here?" Paris ventured.

Grandma nodded. "That's right. And they won't until your hearing tonight."

My ears perked up. "Hearing? What hearing?"

My grandmother rolled her eyes. "Well, I'm not going to just hand over my grandsons for termination. Of course we'll have a hearing."

"What hearing? I've never heard of the family holding any hearings!" It was true. Bombays were more likely to just shoot first and ask the dead body questions later.

"We haven't held a hearing since . . ." She scratched her chin. "Oh, since 1823." She cast a glance at Leonie. "Let's just say it didn't end well."

Oh, great. We were just waiting for some weird witch trial. Maybe we could talk them out of it. I couldn't think. My head ached, and I had this strange aftertaste of yellow mustard.

"What did you hit us with, anyway?" I asked.

"Just some knockout gas. I don't really want to tell all our secrets in front of an outsider and competitor." She turned to Leonie. "No offense, dear."

"Um, none taken?" Leonie responded quietly.

"I just have to figure out a way to punish

you without killing all three of you. I figured time was on my side." She looked at her watch. "Unfortunately I overdid it on the gas and you slept too long." She pushed a button on the wall, and I watched as three hooks on heavy chains came down from the ceiling and clamped on our chairs. I could hear a light humming noise, and I looked down to see the floor open up. We didn't fall, as the chains from the ceiling lowered us to the floor of the room below. Just as the legs of our chairs touched down, the hooks disengaged and retreated into the ceiling and the room above. The ceiling closed up, leaving no trace of the secret room above.

Paris and I looked at each other. Actually I think we were both impressed—and more than a little freaked out—by what had just happened.

"What is this place?" Leonie whispered.

"I don't know," I answered. "But it sounds like we have some chance to get out of this alive."

"'Always look on the bright side of life,' eh?" Leonie gave me a weak smile.

"*Life of Brian*?" Paris asked, and she nodded.

I was getting a little sick of movie quotes. And I was the one who started them. "Someone's coming," I whispered.

I was not at all surprised to see all five members of the Council come into the room and take seats on the dais. Grandma was the last one in, and she made the introduction of Leonie to the others. She did it with a gentleness and politeness that made it seem like we weren't actually tied to chairs about to die.

"You really screwed up this time, Dakota," Troy sneered. I hated that limey bastard.

"Actually, I think you're right." I shouldn't have answered, but I couldn't help myself. "I screwed up by not killing you last time we were here."

"Nice," Paris muttered.

"We haven't decided what to do with you yet, so quit the cowboy swagger, Dak." Dela smiled. Florence, the other European, nodded.

"My life isn't for you to bargain with, Aunt Dela," I snapped. "I'm sick of all this bullshit."

"That's disrespectful, Dak." Lou's face was an alarming shade of red.

"All right, Lou," Grandma said. "We haven't decided what to do. That's what we're here for."

Damn. I really wished I weren't tied up. A hand cannon would've been nice too. Instead all I could do was sit there and bleed.

Troy shrugged. "What's there to decide? Dak didn't follow through on the hit. In fact, he rescued her from us. The bylaws are pretty straightforward."

Ah. So it was the Council we were running from. I guess that cleared up that mystery. Too bad I couldn't celebrate.

Lou nodded. "I agree. We shoot Dak and his lady friend. Paris gets a warning."

"I don't know about that," Dela said. "Those bylaws haven't been changed since the Middle Ages. I think there's some wiggle room here."

Flo spoke up in her French accent: "Dela is right. We have to change with the times."

I looked expectantly at Grandma, but she refused to meet my gaze. The way the Council haggled as if we weren't even there really pissed me off. Grandma said her goal was to buy us some time, but she sure as hell wasn't helping us.

"Either we do as we've always done and follow the letter of the law, or we disband," Lou demanded.

"We've always followed the code. No exceptions. We can't bring back the others we've punished. We can't change things now," Troy argued.

"What about the last traitor?" Lou shouted. "My grandson was terminated for his treachery." He pointed a finger at me. "The same rules have to apply."

I was not too happy to see that his argument was starting to work on the others. I was also not too happy to be compared to Lou's slimy grandson, who tried to turn the whole family in to international authorities last fall.

"Do we get to say anything?" I yelled.

"No," Troy answered. "You betrayed the family. And Paris helped you. I think only the highest penalty should apply. All three of you should pay the price."

Leonie kept quiet, which was probably good. This was her first introduction to the extended family, and I was sure she wouldn't want to make a bad impression.

"You have to vote, Uncle Troy," Paris said. "And it looks like the women are against you."

"Be quiet, Paris!" Grandma snapped. "He's right. I'm not happy about it."

"Well, I'm so sorry to have to inconvenience you, Grandma," I said. "You almost made a mistake with me before. Do you want to make the same mistake again?"

Dela looked sad. "I'm afraid we have no choice, Dak. But I promise you we will change these rules. Unfortunately you'll be dead, but the amendments will benefit your son."

I rolled my eyes. "Oh, that makes me feel much better."

Lou turned away from me. "So, how do we finish it?"

Troy pointed at Leonie. "First, Dak has to complete the job he started. Then we take care of him and Paris."

They were going to make me kill Leonie? Bullshit on that! I wasn't about to do it. It's like that old saw you see in movies where the bad guys make the good guy dig his own grave, and he does it, thinking he's buying himself some time, but in the end he's dead *and* he's done their backbreaking work for them. No way.

"Ha!" I shouted. "I'm not going to do it. You can't make me kill her." What were they going to do? Give me a gun? I'd take them out before they could react.

"Oh, you'll do it, all right." Lou and Troy came down to where I was and untied one of my hands. They took a rod as long as my arm and attached it to a slot in the chair, then secured my arm to the rod. Lou took his Glock and ejected the magazine—meaning there was only one bullet left in the gun. He placed the gun in my hand while Troy used duct tape to secure it. My arm and hand with a gun in it, like it or not, were pointed straight at Leonie.

"Well, I'm not pulling the trigger," I said defiantly. How could they make me do that?

Lou laughed. "It's remote-controlled, boy. I'll actually deploy the trigger. You'll be holding the gun that kills your girlfriend. It's genius, really."

I was starting to sweat. At any moment that sadist could push a button that would blow a large hole in Leonie's head. And I had no control over it.

"*No!*" Paris cried. "Don't make him do it! Don't you people have hearts?" *Attaboy.* Still my wingman—till the bitter end.

I figured I had only one chance. It wouldn't save any of us, but it would make it so I didn't blow my lover's brains out. There was only a split second to act before they figured out what I was doing. I took a deep breath and threw my weight to my right as hard and fast as possible.

It worked. I tipped over. Lou must've pressed the button, because the gun went off as I fell, missing Leonie by inches. My triumph was short-lived, as I now realized I was stuck on the floor, tied to a chair with my arm duct-taped to a rod.

Of course, this wouldn't stop them from killing us. But if they had their heart set on my killing Leonie, it would buy us a few moments while they set me up and loaded the gun again.

"I love you, Leonie," I called out from my awkward position on the floor. I just didn't want her to die without hearing that.

"I love you too, Dak," Leonie said quietly.

"Come on, people!" Paris called out from somewhere behind me. "They're married! Can't you cut them some slack?" I thought that if I ever got out of this I'd do something really nice for Paris. Maybe buy him a book on how to make Harvey Wallbangers, or the entire set of Rat Pack movies. Something like that.

A loud bang came from somewhere behind me. I couldn't see what happened, so I focused on Leonie's face, which happened to be looking at me.

"We would've had a great life together," I said to her.

Leonie smiled. "I know."

Behind me I could hear voices, but I was too caught up in her. She looked beautiful. Glowing, actually. Like an angel. A gorgeous angel. The Madonna.

"Dak," she began.

"You don't have to say it." I wanted to make this as easy as possible for her. She didn't have to prove herself to me.

"I really need to tell you something," she persisted.

"Leonie, it's okay. I understand, or know, or whatever. There's nothing you could say that would affect how I feel for you at this very moment."

"I'm pregnant," Leonie said.

Chapter Thirty-five

Tommy: "Roy, have you got the hammer?"
Roy: "Always got the hammer, Tommy."
— *Death to Smoochy*

I was filled with a feeling I'd never had before. For the first time in my life I was so mind-numbingly happy, I forgot all about where we were. Hell, I didn't mind that the very expensive condoms I kept in my night-stand had failed. In fact, I was happy they had, for the second time in my life. Louis was going to have a baby brother or sister! He'd love that.

"That's enough!" I heard my mother's voice scream behind me. "I've had it with you, Mother!" She sounded angrier than I'd ever heard her before.

Someone was lifting me and my chair upright. Paris and his dad, Uncle Pete, were untying me. I looked to my right and saw Mom's cousins Cali and Montana untying Leonie.

On the dais Lou's kids, York and Georgia, had guns trained on the Council, while Troy and Florence's kids, Burma and Asia, were glowering.

"No one . . . and I mean *no one*," Mom shouted, "pulls a gun on my unborn grand-child!"

I watched in amazement as her brother and cousins nodded. This was a Bombay coup d'etat!

"Consider yourselves in retirement," Burma's crisp English accent admonished.

The five members of the Council faced the greater number of their own children. All eight of them. Without a word they handed their pistols over to York and Georgia. In a split second a new Council had taken over. It was an amazing thing to behold.

"How did you know?" I asked Mom after she spent several minutes fawning all over Leonie.

She turned to look at me with surprise. "Missi called. She told me what happened in Vegas."

Missi popped up beside her, causing me to jump backward. "After you left Lulu told me the whole Council was in Vegas. That was more than I thought you could handle."

I saw Mom's eyebrows go up at the mention of Lulu, but to her credit she didn't ask.

"So I called your mom and mine and Operation Nursing Home commenced earlier than planned."

"Operation Nursing Home?" Paris asked.

"We've been planning to take over the Council for the past few years now," Mom explained. "We knew none of them would ever let go. So Pete and the cousins and I decided it was time for a new regime. We've been wanting to make some changes for a long time."

Leonie slumped into my arms. Apparently she'd had her fill of Bombay family fun for the day.

Paris and I took one of the Jeeps and drove to the airstrip on the island, and in a few hours the three of us were on our private jet en route to home.

We weren't sure if it was safe for Leonie at her house, so we checked her into a suite at the downtown Marriott, and Paris and I headed to my condo to pick up a few things.

We got to my place to find the door wide-open. I didn't ever leave it unlocked, let alone standing ajar. Quietly we slipped inside and locked the door behind us. Voices came from the hallway. They sounded like two men. I reached inside my coat closet and pulled out the hidden shotgun and handgun I kept there.

I pointed to Paris, silently telling him to take one side of the hallway. He nodded and we crept toward my bedroom. After making eye contact for a second, we burst into the room, guns blazing (which looked really cool, I'd bet).

Neil and Anders grinned sheepishly from their places on the floor. They were wrist-deep in my underwear drawer, and the whole image was something I wanted desperately to forget.

"What the *hell*?" I said, keeping the shotgun trained on Anders's midsection. "Doc Savages, I presume?" I asked in my best James Bond voice.

"Heh, heh." Neil laughed nervously. "Well, you see . . ." He looked at Anders, who conveniently shrugged.

Turned out our friends, the Mossad and CIA operatives, were looking for Paris's blackmail photos of them. They were both up for promotions, and Paris's threats of the photos were more than they could bear. So, they hired a couple of real lowlifes to break into my place, using my old obsession as a taunt to throw me off track.

And while I was relieved to hear that Doc Savage was no longer a threat, we were still pissed off at our old college buddies.

So it was little more than twenty-four hours

later that Neil and Anders found themselves naked, bound, and gagged in an S and M den in Paraguay, under the not-so-tender ministrations of a three-hundred-pound tranny dominatrix named Earl.

You just couldn't put a price on the digital photos Earl sent back. Oh, we would never send them to their office. Of course, they wouldn't know that.

Epilogue

"I wish I could do something about this. But I can't. But I can promise you two things. One: I'll always look this good. Two: I'll never give up on you . . . ever."

—Hellboy, *Hellboy*

"Just sign here, Mrs. Bombay," Eli Morgan said, pointing his knockoff Montblanc pen at a dotted line.

Leonie looked at me for a moment. Was she hesitating?

"You don't have to do this," I said, "if you're not ready."

She looked at the now frowning Mr. Morgan, then down at her round tummy.

"Yes. Yes, I do."

"I mean"—I took a deep breath and repeated what I'd told her in private a half hour ago—"we could find a way of tying the two family businesses together."

Leonie laughed and shook her head. "Yeah. Like that would work."

She went ahead and signed her name, then

handed the forms over to the confused banker. Selling Crummy's had been her idea. I thought maybe we could tie in the funeral home with the assassination business, but we never did figure out how. Oh, well.

"And what business are you in, Mr. Bombay?" Morgan frowned at me again.

"Oh," I said with a grin at my wife, "I'm in marketing."

Nine months later Leonie gave birth to a perfect little girl we named Sofia. You might think we were breaking the rules of place names in the Bombay family, but just look at a map of Bulgaria.

Louis was thrilled with the new house we bought just down the street from Gin and Diego. The condo association had kind of frowned on the fact that I'd had break-ins. Go figure.

At any rate, the kids needed a house. Louis loved his new bedroom, backyard, and chemistry lab in the basement. He was doing great in school, and even won the Boy Scouts' pine wood derby. The judges suspected something was up (and they were right), but couldn't prove anything. I'll never tell.

Leonie lives in semiretirement. She helps me with the occasional assignment, just to keep her skills from getting rusty. Her specialty? Well, she came up with this method of embalming someone while they're still alive. I think there might be some issues with her childhood there, but she seems happy.

As for the Bombays, we're still doing business but with a few changes. The new and improved Council relaxed a lot of the stricter rules from the past, making us all sleep a little bit better at night. And the number of jobs was limited to two per year, and not within the same six months of each other. Of course, there might be circumstances in the future that would take exception to that, but you'd have that.

The new Council kept a lot of the same traditions, but seemed to have a softer approach to things. And it all seemed to be working out pretty smoothly.

What happened to the old Council members? Oh, they were still around. Just retired. Mom, Pete, and the others put them in a nice little maximum-security nursing home in Greenland, where the staff consists of large, non–English speaking, angry Inuit women. I heard that Lou tried to escape last month after turning his wooden ice cream spoon into a shiv. He spent a month in solitary, sharing a locked room with an incontinent retired sumo wrestler who liked to give "big hugs."

And me? Do I miss the old days of the free-wheeling Dakster? Not at all. My small but lethal family is enough to keep me on my toes for the rest of my life. And in this family, you never know how long that may be.

Get a special sneak peek at

ALIBI IN HIGH HEELS

by National Readers' Choice Award Winner
Gemma Halliday

Currently I had two vices: Mexican food and Mexican men. Thanks to an early-morning shooting on Olympic Boulevard that had my boyfriend, Detective Jack Ramirez, crawling out of bed at the crack of dawn, I couldn't indulge in the latter. Which left me with the former, in the form of a grande nachos supremo at The Whole Enchilada in Beverly Hills. And I had to admit the gooey cheddar and salsa–induced semi-orgasm I was experiencing was almost as good as what I'd had planned for Ramirez this morning.

Almost.

"Tell me again about the sex?" my best friend, Dana, asked, leaning both of her elbows on the table across from me.

I grinned. I couldn't help it. After spending the night with Ramirez, there was nothing I could do to wipe that sucker off. "It was hot."

Dana licked her lips. "How hot?"

I picked up a stray jalapeño from my plate. "Ten of these and you still wouldn't even be close."

Dana sighed, then started fanning herself with a napkin imprinted with a dancing cactus. "You know, it's been so long, I can hardly even remember what a one-jalapeño night would be like."

Dana's current boyfriend du jour was Ricky Montgomery, who played the hunky gardener on the hit TV show *Magnolia Lane*. Amazingly, my fated-to-short-term-romance friend had actually taken a vow of monogamy with Ricky, which, thus far, had lasted a record nine months. I was pretty proud of Dana. Especially considering that as soon as shooting had ended for the *Magnolia Lane* season, Ricky had flown off to Croatia to do a film with Natalie Portman. Ricky said the script was amazing and had Oscar written all over it. Dana said she was investing in a battery-powered rabbit and praying they wrapped quickly.

"So, when is Ricky coming back?" I asked around a bite of cool sour cream and hot salsa. I'm telling you, pure heaven.

"Three more weeks. I'm just not sure I can make it, Maddie. This is the longest I've ever gone without sex."

I raised an eyebrow. "Ever?"

Dana nodded vigorously. "Since ninth grade."

Wow. I think in ninth grade I was still negotiating with Bobby Preston over second base.

"Why don't you just go visit him?"

She shook her head. "Can't. The set's in a military zone. They needed all sorts of permits and things just to be there. Booty call isn't exactly on the list of approved reasons."

"Sorry."

"Thanks." Dana sipped at her iced tea, giving my jalapeño a longing look.

"If it makes you feel any better, last night was the

only action I've gotten in weeks, too." Not to mention that I was currently substituting a morning of naked sheet wrestling with rice and beans.

Dana sighed again, the kind that only blonde-haired, blue-eyed wanna-be actresses can conjure up without sounding fake. "Not really, but thanks for trying."

"Hey, how about we go for pedis? A fresh coat of toenail polish always makes me feel better. I've got an appointment at Fernando's in twenty minutes. Wanna join me?"

Dana shook her head, her ponytail whipping her cheeks. "Sorry, no can do. I've got an audition at one. I'm reading for the part of a streetwalker on that new David E. Kelly show. I can so nail this one."

I looked her up and down, taking in her denim micro-mini, three-inch heels, and pink crop top. I hated to admit it, but she so could.

After I'd fully consumed my nacho supremeo, stopping just short of actually licking the plate, Dana and I walked down Santa Monica, making a right on Beverly, where my little red Jeep was parked at the end of the busy street in front of Fernando's salon. Normally actually *walking* two blocks in L.A. was an unheard of phenomenon, but this was prime Beverly Hills shopping territory. The boutiques lining the street held windows full of designer purses, thousand-dollar tank tops, and Italian leather shoes with stitching so small, you'd swear it was the work of leprechauns.

Dana paused in front of the Bellissimo Boutique. "Ohmigod, Mads! Are those yours?" She pointed to a pair of red patent leather Mary Janes with a black kitten heel.

I grinned so wide I felt my cheeks crack (and this time it had nothing to do with Ramirez *or* gooey, cheddar-laden chips).

Last year I had a moment of minor Internet fame, which prompted a trendy local boutique to ask me to design a line of shoes for them, called High Heels Seduction. Not surprisingly, I squealed, squeaked, and generally jumped around like a six-year-old minus her Ritalin. And then things got even better when the first pair of Maddie Springer originals was sold to an up-and-coming young actress who just happened to be wearing them when she got arrested outside the Twilight Club on Sunset Boulevard for drug possession. Suddenly my shoes were all over *Entertainment Tonight*, *Access Hollywood*, and even CNN. I got calls from the hippest shops in L.A. and Orange County, all clamoring to stock my High Heels Seduction.

Including the Bellissimo Boutique.

"Yep," I said, beaming with a pride usually reserved for mothers sporting *Student of the Month* bumper stickers. "Those are my latest. You like?"

"I love! Oh, I so want a pair. Hey, you think you could do something for me to wear to the premiere of Ricky's movie when you get back from Paris?"

Oh, did I forget to mention the best part of being a *real* fashion designer?

Once my shoes hit CNN, I got a call from Jean Luc Le Croix, the hottest new European fashion designer, asking me, little ol' me, to come show my shoes in his fall runway collection at Paris Fashion Week.

Paris!

I had truly died and gone to heaven. Not surprisingly, I'd first had a mild heart attack, then did a repeat of the six-year-old-Ritalin-addict thing. I was set to fly out next week and still hadn't come down off the high.

"*Oui, oui, mademoiselle*. What would you like?" I asked.

"Oh, I totally know what I want! I saw the cutest pair of wedge-heeled sandals on J. Lo at the MTV awards. They were, like, black with this little trail of sequins going down the . . ." But Dana trailed off, her eyes fixing on a point just over my shoulder.

"What?"

I spun around and stood rooted to the spot. A little yellow sports car was careening down Beverly at Daytona 500 speeds. It sideswiped a Hummer, narrowly missing a woman carrying a Dolce shopping bag, then bounced back into traffic, tires squealing.

"Ohmigod, Maddie," Dana said, her voice going high and wild. "Look out!"

I watched in horror as the little car cut across two lanes, jumping the curb and accelerating.

Straight toward me.

'Scuse Me While I Kill This Guy

Leslie Langtry

To most people, Gin Bombay is an ordinary single mom. But this mom is from a family of top secret assassins. Somewhere between leading a Girl Scout troop for her kindergartner and keeping their puppy from destroying the furniture, Gin has to take out a new target. Except this target has an incredibly hot Australian bodyguard who knows just how to make her weak in the knees. But with a mole threatening to expose everything, Gin doesn't have much time to let her hormones do the happy dance. She's got to find the leak and clear her assignment…or she'll end up next on the Bombay family hit list.

ISBN 10: 0-8439-5933-9
ISBN 13: 978-0-8439-5933-8

To order a book or to request a catalog call:
1-800-481-9191
This book is also available at your local bookstore, or you can check out our Web site **www.dorchesterpub.com** where you can look up your favorite authors, read excerpts, or glance at our discussion forum to see what people have to say about your favorite books.